Glass Bay

An Emily Jade Thriller

Sean Monaghan

Glass Bay

An Emily Jade Thriller

by Sean Monaghan

Copyright © 2018 Sean Monaghan

All rights reserved.

Published by Triple V Publishing

Cover illustration
© Claudioarnese | Dreamstime

Discover other titles by this author at:
www.seanmonaghan.com

ISBN: 1985247720
ISBN–13: 978-1985247727

This novel is a work of fiction. All characters, places and incidents described in this publication are used ficticiously, or are entirely fictional.

No part of this publication may be reproduced or transmitted, in any form, or by any means, except for fair use by reviewers or with written permission from the publisher. www.triplevpublishing.com

ALSO BY SEAN MONAGHAN

EMILY JADE THRILLERS
Big Sur

STANDALONE THRILLERS
Big Sur
Ice Fracture
The Room
The Courier

CONTEMPORARY NOVELS
This is the Perfect Way to Wake
Steel Wagons

KARNISH RIVER NAVIGATIONS SERIES
Arlchip Burnout
Night Operations
Guest House Izarra
Canal Days
Persephone Quest

SCIENCE FICTION
Asteroid Jumpers
The City Builders
Athena Setting
The Cly
Gretel
Rotations
Habitat

THE HIDDEN DOME TRILOGY
The Tunnel
The Deluge
The Eye

COLLECTIONS
Listen, You!
Back from Vermont
Balance i
Balance ii
Balance iii
*Un*Balanced

ANTHOLOGIES (Editor)
Dieselpunk
Hospital
A Butterfly in China

Glass Bay

CHAPTER ONE

Rich Cooper strode toward the old wharf bar. The sound of the late high-tide waves slapping against the concrete seawall mingled with the strains of Johnny Cash drifting from the bar's cranky old jukebox.

Overhead, stars winked. Out across the black of the vast Atlantic, Rich saw the eerie glow of full white rainclouds lit by the soon-to-rise moon.

Ships plied the horizon. Some had blinking lights. The sight reminded Rich of his mother, Edith, off on her cruise to England and the Mediterranean.

In his back pocket Rich had a printout of his air ticket. He smiled to himself. He would be surprising her in Italy, when the ship called at

Naples.

A birthday present for her. After all, it had been a tough eighteen months.

First his father, then his sister, Toni. Heart attack. Mugging.

Frankly, Rich was surprised that his mother had the energy to get on the ship. A good thing. He admired her courage and tenacity.

Stopping at the door to the bar, Rich took a breath.

The faded sign along the frontage read *Bernie's Rest*. Three of five spotlights still worked, shining at the sign. Paint peeled from the plastered cinderblock walls, revealing generations of layers.

Some of the wooden window framing was warped. Bernie's daughter, Claire, the current owner, had used grout and plaster to take care of the worst of the gaps.

Once the bar had been a haven for tourists. Before back-to-back storms tore the community to pieces. Swamps where there had been subdivisions. Barren sandy ground that had once been lush with watermelons and oranges.

Homes saturated and floated off their foundations.

Taking another breath, Rich stepped to the bar. Even after all of this, the sea air still felt invigorating. Elemental.

Perhaps that was why he'd stuck around. Doing what he could with his money and skills to help people out. At least, those families who'd had the will to stick around.

"Hey you!" someone called out as Rich went

inside. Jodie Clemons. Old flame. Divorced three times since. Still pretty and energetic. Wearing her hair in a short, dyed-black bob.

Rich waved back. She was alone. He pointed to the bar. She nodded, holding up a highball glass. Rich knew she would have a half-shot of vodka with soda water and a twist of lime. He headed to the bar.

Jodie smiled and bent her head back to her phone. She tapped at the screen.

The bar smelled of pine, rather than beer. Enough space for a dozen regular tables, a few tall tables and a darts and pool area. The jukebox flashed and flickered in the corner. Johnny Cash faded out, replaced by Dolly Parton. Nothing from this century in *Bernie's Rest*.

Aside from Jodie, there were just four others.

Two young tourists, probably European, wearing matching hiking boots and jackets, one male, one female. Blonde as the soon-to-rise moon.

The others were Claire, behind the bar, with a spray bottle–which explained the pine scent–and a cloth, and Big Ed.

Claire wiped at the bar. Big Ed played pool alone at the torn and faded table. He gave Rich a nod.

Rich returned it. He ordered Jodie's drink and a Heineken for himself.

"You sure you're good?" Claire said. "Heard you're flying out."

"I'll be back in a week," he said.

"I'll keep your seat warm." Claire pushed the drinks across the bar and returned to her cleaning. As he picked them up, she said, "Don't you go getting any ideas about Jodie, you hear? She's vulnerable."

"When is she not?"

"Well, that rat Bradley ditched her a couple days ago."

"Bradley?"

"Yeah. Who knew?"

"Thanks."

Rich set the drinks down on Jodie's table.

"I guess Claire gave you my current life story?" Jodie said.

"Well." Rich glanced back at the bar where Claire continued polishing. "She gave me a precis."

Jodie smiled. "I like how you say that word. Precis."

Rich kept his hands on the drinks. "How many have you had?"

Jodie reached over, putting her fingers around his on the glass. Her hand was warm.

"This," she said, "Will be my third."

"Okay then. It's nice to see you." He shifted his hand and she let go so he could let go.

Jodie took the glass. "You're my rock, you know?"

"You've mentioned before."

"You're leaving me, though."

"A week. I'll be right back."

"I'll look forward to it." Jodie took a sip from the vodka and soda.

Rich tasted the Heineken. Cool and refreshing. Exactly what he needed. Right away he felt it trying to run through him. An age-old bladder problem.

"Gotta use the men's room," he told Jodie. "If I'm not back in five, send help."

"Will do."

Rich went through the door marked 'Buoys', next to the door marked 'Gulls'.

It was the last time anyone ever saw Rich Cooper. Alive, anyway.

CHAPTER TWO

Emily Jade–Jade to her friends, and her enemies–sat in a quaint little diner off the highway just outside of Fernville City. Morning sun poured through grimy windows. The view across the highway nothing more interesting than a run-down independent gas station and a stand of pines. A sign on the roadside warned of deer.

Inside, gingham table cloths complemented bunting and tied back curtains with frills and bunching. Each table had a hand-made wooden rack holding the glass condiment bottles.

A few others sat in the diner. A trucker with a battered 49ers baseball cap sat on a stool at the counter. In a booth near the back, an elderly couple sat, here for the bottomless coffee. A businessman with an impeccable suit, pressed shirt and maroon tie sat at one of the window tables. One hand on his phone, the businessman dug into his Big Breakfast with a fork in the other hand.

A young waitress brought a coffee pot across to Jade. "What can I get you?" The waitress had a ring in her nose and enough kohl around her eyes to paint out the sun. Maybe sixteen years old.

"Give me minute," Jade said. "I'm meeting a friend."

"Big Breakfast's good." The waitress's nametag identified her as Chakana. "If you want enough food for a couple of days."

Jade glanced at the businessman. "He's making short work of his."

Chakana looked over. She rolled her eyes. "In here every day. Eats maybe two bacon rashes and half a biscuit. Drinks about six coffees. Watches my tush too much." Chakana shrugged. "Leaves a good tip, so who am I to complain?"

"You, if he's bothering you."

"I can handle myself. So long as it's only his eyes. If he ever gets handsy I'll deck him." Chakana poured coffee into the empty cup on Jade's table.

"Thanks." Jade managed a smile. Chakana could take care of herself.

"Haven't seen you around," Chakana said.

"Passing through," Jade said. How often had she had the same conversation? How many waitresses in greasy spoons had said some variation on 'haven't seen you around'.

"Who passes through this place? It's not like it's on the way to anywhere."

"Just some business out on the island." Jade

took a sip from the coffee. Bitter and old. She took another sip. At least it was warm. She reached for a sachet of creamer in the re-purposed peanut butter jar.

"Tollis Island?" Chakana said. "Nothing going on out there these days. Unless you're buying up property at six cents an acre."

Jade smiled. "Maybe that's what I'm doing."

She'd checked the island on the maps before coming down. Tollis Island was a sickle-shaped sand bar fifteen miles long, five miles across at its widest. Part of the long chain of the outer banks.

High enough that there was some development. Low enough that storms made permanent structures vulnerable.

The island's best feature was Glass Bay. A wide piece of calm water enclosed in the hook of the sickle. Popular with weekend sailors and hobby fishers alike.

"Huh," Chakana said. "If you're buying, I've got a bridge in Brooklyn I can sell you too. Got the deed right out back."

"How about just a cheese omelet with a side salad."

"Sure thing. You want sausage with that?"

"Yes please."

"Swiss, Old English or cheddar?"

Jade answered each of the next half-dozen questions as Chakana built the meal. She didn't take any notes.

"Got it. Might be fifteen minutes. Karl went on a bender last night, so he's pretty bleary."

"He's your cook?"

"Yeah. And part-owner. I probably shouldn't tell the customers when he's under the weather."

"Happen often?"

"Every other day." Chakana took a step away. "Now, you just holler if you need that coffee topped up."

"Will do."

A car pull up in the diner's gravel lot. A beat-up white Prius. Dusty and battered, the car looked like it had recently survived a demolition derby. The Prius parked in next to the black BMW that Jade guessed belonged to the businessman, or the elderly couple.

The Prius's driver got out and Jade knew right away he was her contact.

A gangly twenty-something wearing jeans, a tee shirt with a band logo and a black leather jerkin. He had a dark-blue backpack slung over one shoulder. On the highway, a black pick-up swished by.

Jade herself wore comfortable black skinny jeans, black tee shirt, boots and she had her black jacket lying on the booth's seat next to her. She knew that the all-black outfit gave her a certain look, but today she was okay with that.

The new arrival came in through the diner's wood and glass door. He spotted Jade and made a beeline.

"Emily?" he said.

"Sebastien." Jade pointed at the seat across from her. "Most people call me Jade."

"All right. You're smaller than I thought. You're here to help me find my uncle?"

"That's what the message said. Richard

Cooper." She let the comment on her size go. Five-two and a hundred and two pounds. People tended to underestimate her, and that suited Jade fine.

"He's been missing three weeks. His mother's beside herself."

"You didn't go to the police?"

"Sure we did. But that's a whole other story."

"Why don't you tell it?"

Sebastien gave a nod. "Where to start?"

"I find," Emily said, and took another sip from the coffee. It was growing on her. "That the beginning usually works."

Another nod. "Of course."

CHAPTER THREE

The diner hummed. At the next table over, Chakana gathered a tip and cleared away plates. The elderly couple sipped away at their coffee.

Out on the highway a chunky pickup towed a shiny white boat on a trailer. A few cars backed up behind.

Across from Jade, Sebastien ran through the facts quickly.

His uncle, Richard Cooper, had vanished a year back. It had been a month before anyone realized that he'd gone missing. Police had become involved. A lack of details slowed them down. Eventually they dropped the case.

"Which is not what they actually call it," Sebastien said.

"More like, 'continuing to pursue new facts as they come to light'?"

"Something like that." Sebastien looked up as Chakana came by with the coffee pot. "Please,"

Sebastien said, pushing his cup closer.

Chakana smiled. Jade noticed now that she had braces. Blue rubber bands holding them in place.

"You're who she was waiting for?" Chakana said as she poured. "She your mom?"

Sebastien laughed. "I'm not that young," he said.

"And I'm not that old," Jade said with a laugh. She knew that anyone beyond their mid-thirties looked *old* to anyone under twenty.

At thirty-three, Jade kept herself toned and in good shape. She ate right, got enough sleep and studied. And despite all that, time caught up. She could see the beginnings of lines at the corners of her eyes. She could feel a slight slackness in her arms. And despite a concentrated exercise regime, she knew that her recovery times were gradually increasing.

Chakana looked almost mortified. "I'm sorry. I just thought I saw a family resemblance."

Jade and Sebastien looked right at each other. Jade didn't see anything familiar at all.

"She's my older sister," Sebastien said, looking over at Chakana.

"I knew it!"

"Did you order yet, sis?" Sebastien said.

"The usual," Jade said, not quite sure if she liked Sebastien or not. He was sharp, which was something.

"Good," Sebastien said. "Can you make that two?"

"Coming right up." Chakana left, almost beating a hasty retreat.

"Sister," Jade said. "You should just walk out now. While you're still marginally ahead."

It wasn't like she needed the work. Practically pro-bono.

Except that Mueller had said it was worth looking into. Another clue in a much bigger mystery.

Sebastien took a sip from his coffee. He grimaced. Took a breath and took a deeper drink. Instead of responding to Jade's suggestion, he said, "We got a local private investigator. Lasted a couple of months. His bill was... well, we didn't get change from ten grand."

"Hefty. Results?"

"Lots of documents. A few interviews. Sightings. Possibilities. The guy drank too much too, often—the investigator I mean, not my uncle."

"Okay."

"But the documentation was clear. I think he had a good clerk. Typed up everything from his scrawl. H paid her well. You know the kind of thing. Horrible person, but really good a connecting the dots. The clerk's the opposite. Smart, but didn't have his insight. They made a good team. I don't think he realized how good he had it."

"Maybe I need to talk to her. The clerk."

"Maisie Souther. I can get you her number. She..." Sebastien blinked. Turned to look out the window.

Jade followed his gaze. A pick-up drove by. Slow.

Black. Same one that had gone by just

moments before Sebastien had arrived.

"You know them?" Jade said.

"Little bit."

"Causing problems?"

"Little bit." Sebastien nodded.

"You might need to explain that too."

Sebastien kept watching until the pick-up slipped out of view behind some of the old pines along the highway's shoulder.

Sebastien pursed his lips.

Chakana arrived with Jade's steaming breakfast. "Sorry it took so long," Chakana said.

Jade was sure no more than a couple of minutes had passed. As the plate of food slipped across the table, the heavenly smell wrapped around her nose.

"Oh man," Sebastien said. "Is that what I ordered?"

"Cook's working on it now," Chakana said. "Almost there."

"Thanks."

As she ate, Jade kept an eye on the highway. The black pick-up didn't cruise by again.

CHAPTER FOUR

Sebastien's place was nothing more than a two-room shack off at dirt road that ran three miles from the highway. Old pines grew in the sandy ground, their scent filling Jade's rental Ram as she followed Sebastien's Prius.

Jade had paid for both their breakfasts, and left a decent tip for Chakana. Sebastien had seemed grateful, though still willing to pay.

Seeing the shack, Jade figured he could use every saving.

The rental's big tires rumbled through the rutted surface as Jade pulled up out front of the shack. An old Trans-Am lay windowless and rotting next to the building. The car might have once had a red paint job.

Inside the shack, the kitchen-dining-bedroom-living room smelled of too many spaghetti and meatballs meals. A faded crocheted blanket lay across the fold-out bed and the wooden table had two mis-matched chairs. No carpet, but there were some rugs scattered over the floorboards.

"Bathroom's out back," Sebastien said. "If you need it."

Jade figured she might hold on. Ragged lace curtains hung over some windows. She could see gaps between the frame and the backdoor by the bench.

The second room, which Sebastien told her he'd converted from a bedroom to a study, looked like something out of a conspiracy theory show. Newspaper clippings and photographs pinned to the wall. With maps, notes and hand-drawn sketches.

"Not what you expected, right?" Sebastien said. "You take a look around and decide on my sanity. I'll make some coffee."

"Already had coffee," Jade said.

"Well I did mean for me." Sebastien had an actual electric kettle, which he filled with water from the faucet on the bench. He plugged the kettle in and it began hissing.

Jade looked over the gathered documents. At one end of the room stood a table under a grimy window. Beyond, an old bathtub lay out in the scrubby weeds at the edge of the woods. Jade realized that the tub was still in use. Sebastien had to clean up somewhere.

How had the family had come up with ten thousand dollars for the ineffective P.I.?

Papers and folders littered the table. A bare desklamp pointed down.

"So?" Sebastien said. "What do you think?"

"Where's the string?" Jade said.

"What?"

"Shouldn't you have lengths of string or wool? Joined by pins across this wall. You know, so you can quickly see the links?"

Sebastien's eyes widened. "Do you think I should?"

Jade put her hand on his upper arm. "I'm kidding."

"You do think I'm mad, don't you."

"On the evidence so far, the jury's out."

Sebastien stepped into the room. The floor creaked. "I started out neat and tidy on the table," he said. "But as I got more and more stuff, I had to spread out. Onto the floor, then onto the wall. I couldn't hold all this in my head at once."

Sounds came from around the cabin. The whisper of wind through the trees and the distant passage of cars on the highway. The electric kettle clicked off.

"Won't be a minute." Sebastien slipped back to the other room.

Jade went to the board. One of the photos showed a pair of men clearly on a hunting trip. Standing on a ridge with rolling, tree-covered hills behind. Plaid shirts, beaten up, camouflage pattern baseball caps and four days of beard growth.

Someone–presumably Sebastien–had drawn a circle around the man on the left. Middle-aged, blonde hair, brown eyes. He had short white scar on his left cheek, just over the bone.

Jade smelled coffee, heard the same creak in the floor. "Your uncle?" she said without turning. She tapped the circled man in the photo.

"No," Sebastien said. "One of his Eagle Scout buddies. Coleman D. Gardner. From Charleston. West Virginia."

"Yes, I know where Charleston is."

"Sorry."

"It's fine. Keep feeding me information. Eagle Scouts?"

"That's what they called themselves. Kind of a joke, really. They thought it was hilarious."

I bet. "Who's the other guy? Not your uncle?"

"Don't know who he is. One of the leads I haven't gotten anywhere with yet."

"All right. What about this map?" Jade pointed to a sketched map of Tollis Island. The island lay just a few miles away. Part of the outer banks along the North Carolina coast. The map highlighted an inland bay tagged 'Glass Bay'.

"Other maps are either cluttered or don't have enough detail. I needed to be able to picture it in my mind with just the right details."

"All right." As Jade turned to the next document that had attracted her attention, she heard a change in the sounds from outside.

A vehicle. Still a half a mile off, or more. But coming fast.

"You expecting someone?"

Sebastien shook his head. "Stay here."

He put the coffee down on top of a folder on the table. There was no other space.

Jade followed him out to the other room. Sebastien crouched at the bench, reaching into the cupboards below.

"Sebastien?"

He came up holding an old Remington

shotgun.

"Hey," Jade said. "What? It's a long time since I've been to North Carolina, but I don't recall that being the way to greet new arrivals."

"Stay here," he said again and headed for the door.

CHAPTER FIVE

The sound of the vehicle continued to grow. Jade stood near Sebastien's bench. Tidy, with a basil plant growing in a pot on the windowsill. She could just smell the sweet scent of the leaves.

And there was Sebastien heading to the door, carrying a shotgun.

Complete contrast.

He'd said to stay where she was. She followed him across to the door anyway. He held the shotgun with the barrels pointing down.

The sound of crunching gravel came from right outside the shack.

The vehicle. Pulling up.

From somewhere in the distance a dog barked.

Sebastien went to the window to the left of the entry door. He peered around.

"Do you know who it is?" Jade said.

"Hush."

Jade moved around, back from the window,

and came up on the other side. She watched through the threadbare curtains.

The black pick-up stood out front.

Four men got out.

All of them wore casual jeans and tee shirts. Jade spotted one that proclaimed *Rolling Stones - 1993*, with the lips and tongue logo.

All four men carried guns.

As Jade watched, one of the men holstered his gun and walked to her Ram. He took a long blade from another holster and proceeded to slash the rear right tire.

"I don't like these guys much," Jade said. She went across the window to the door.

Sebastien grabbed her arm. "Wait."

"No. He's wrecking my car." Through the window she saw the guy move to the front right tire. He slashed it too. The Ram settled, tilting.

"He's not going to stop." Sebastien kept a firm grip on her arm. "And if you go out there, they'll shoot."

"Sebastien!" one of the men called. "Heard you might have gotten some help. We'd like to discourage that."

"By help," Jade said to Sebastien, "I guess he's referring to me."

A nod.

"Sebastien!" Another shout. "Tell you what. We'll give you to the count of ten."

"They won't wait," Sebastien said.

"I get that. They might count, but they'll also circle around so you can't flee."

"That's right."

"You've had problems with these guys

before?"

"Yes."

"And they are...?"

Sebastien frowned. "The Maeberry family. Doug, Bud and Joe."

"There are four." Jade moved to the window again. Three tires down now and the guy was moving toward the last.

"The little guy, to the left," Sebastien said. "He's Ealing Cooper. Works for them."

"Relation?"

Another shout. "Starting now. One."

"A very distant relation. Four or five times removed. My Uncle Rich used to have Ealing's mom over for summer barbeques back in the day."

"Two!"

"Is that detail on the wall?"

"Yes it... uh-oh."

Jade saw it too. The big guy doing the counting retrieved a brown glass bottle from the back of the pick-up.

Rags dangled from the bottle's mouth.

Only the three of them visible out front now.

"We should go," Sebastien said.

One of the others took a bottle too. The third–the one with the knife–took out a lighter.

"Three!"

"Give me the gun," Jade said.

"Not going to happen."

"Suit yourself." Jade turned away from the window. She went to the kitchen bench and found a steak knife in the cluttered drawer.

"Four!" A slow count. These guys knew what

they were doing.

The backdoor wouldn't budge. She pulled on the handle again.

"Yeah," Sebastien called. "That's been stuck for a couple of months."

"Useful." It would have to be a window.

"Five!"

The front window shattered. The bottle landed. Didn't break.

It rolled, trailing burning rags.

CHAPTER SIX

Flames flickered from the rags. The stink of oily smoke. It curled up into the cabin.

Sebastien moved fast. He stomped on the burning rags.

Already the lace curtains were blazing. Little patches of fire spurted across the rugs.

But the bottle hadn't broken.

Jade darted over. She stepped on the burning parts of the rugs.

She grabbed the crocheted blanket from the fold-out bed. She beat at the burning curtain with the blanket.

She was making headway when she heard the guy outside shout, "Six!"

Through the window gap she saw the second bottle. Spinning in the air.

Flames dripped from the burning rags.

"Look out!" Sebastien shouted.

Still spinning, the bottle hit the floor.

The bottle shattered. Flames burst through the room.

Jade turned away. A wave of heat rolled over her. She heard her hair sizzling.

Sebastien screamed.

The stench of oily smoke filled the room. Jade raced for where she'd seen him.

The initial flames died quickly. Volatile fuel consumed. Other parts of the room burned.

Sebastien staggered. Clothes aflame.

Jade tackled him. They thumped on the floor.

Slapping at the flames, Jade rolled him over.

From outside came a shout of, "Seven."

Jade kept rolling Sebastien. The flames diminished. Sebastien moaned.

The room was well ablaze now. Old furniture dry and combustible.

But the flames Sebastien's clothes were out

"Move," Jade said. She dragged Sebastien along.

He got his hands and knees going. Scrabbled along with her. He coughed.

Jade's throat felt raw from the smoke.

She made for the second room. Already the flames had traveled. The licked at Sebastien's documents.

As she came through the door the wall with the photos and sketches exploded with flame.

The fire grew loud. Snaps and pops. And a roaring.

She shoved Sebastien ahead. Toward the table. To the window.

Sebastien staggered. Collapsed.

He had holes in his shirt. Marks on his skin.

Blisters. Red and glistening.

Smoke rolled through the room. Jade crouched to Sebastien. And clearer air.

"We have to go out the window," she said.

Sebastien coughed.

"Stick with me," she told him.

Jade stood to the tabletop. She grabbed the desklamp. Swung it at the window.

The glass shattered. Shards slapped her arms.

Jade dragged the lamp's body along the window frame. Breaking out as much glass as she could.

"Time to go," she said. The guy was probably still out front, counting.

And the other guy out back.

Just waiting for them.

Jade crouched. She grabbed Sebastien by his leather jerkin. Hauled him to his feet.

Pushed him to the window.

Flames licked through the doorway. Across the floor. Ashes floated.

Sebastien tumbled out the window.

Jade jumped out right after him.

To find herself staring into the barrel of a small pistol.

CHAPTER SEVEN

From the pines nearby a bird chirruped. The trees swayed in the breeze.

Standing close to the rickety cabin, Jade could feel the heat from the fire.

The pistol stayed right in front of her. The guy holding it looked young. Barely shaving. A look of forced-determination on his face.

The fire crackled. Another window banged. Shattering. From the heat. Shards tinkled to the floor.

Her eyes watered. She coughed.

She'd dropped the knife when she'd grabbed the blanket. The old joke about bringing a knife to a gunfight wouldn't even apply.

"Stay where you are," the guy said. He kept the gun leveled at her. Both hands on the weapon.

Good technique. Jade watched him carefully.

The guy was young. Maybe twenty-three. He had lanky hair and wore a tee-shirt emblazoned with the name *Chris Cornell*. A silhouette Chris's face peering off to the side.

"He's hurt," Jade said. "We need an ambulance."

The guy laughed. "Not going to happen."

"I'm hurt too." Jade coughed again. She bent forward. Kept coughing.

Over the fire she could hear the others coming around the side of the house.

She didn't have long.

Another cough. She took a lurching step forward.

"Stay where–"

It was too late. Jade swung her arm up. Hit his hands.

With a whipping twist, she pulled the gun back. Over the top of his wrists. The guy screamed. He let go of the gun.

His thumbs cracked. He screamed louder.

Jade got hold of the gun. Turned it on him. She shoved him back.

The pistol was a little Glock. Like a police issue. Light, and with a full magazine. Thirteen shots.

Jade fired two across the side of the shack. Into the ground. The gunshot sounds echoed around the trees.

"You won't get away with this," the guy said.

Jade shot him in the thigh. He went down screaming.

"Jade!" Sebastien said. Croaked. His voice sounded raw.

"Can you move?" she said.

"Yes."

"We need to leave." Jade kept the gun aimed at the corner of the shack. She hoped she'd frightened the other guys off with her shots into the ground.

Maybe not.

"And go where?" Sebastien said.

The guy lay screaming and clutching at his leg.

"Back around the house," Jade said. She realized they'd lost the shotgun. Would have been useful now that the shooting had started.

"Where to? They've got us cut off. You shot him."

"Focus on getting us out of here."

"I know a way," Sebastien said. "Come on."

He ran off.

Not around the house. Toward the bathtub.

"Wait!" Jade shouted.

Too late. He was already too exposed.

Jade fired again into the ground. Trying to keep the others at bay.

She backed after Sebastien.

The fire leapt from the windows. From the loose eaves.

In moments the blaze would have consumed the whole shack. Jade hoped the flames didn't reach the woods. It could turn into a conflagration.

She kept moving. She could hear Sebastien crashing through the weeds.

Jade risked a glance.

He was almost at the trees.

She heard a single shot.

Sebastien jerked at the same moment.

He slumped to the ground.

CHAPTER EIGHT

Jade stared across the grassy area for a moment. She saw a crow dart from the top of one of the nearby pines. The crackling sound of the fire continued.

Sebastien was down.

She almost ran to him.

And that would make her a target too.

Stupid.

Stepping around the blaze, Jade emptied the Glock's clip.

Precise. Measured.

She winged two of the guys. No sign of the fourth.

Jade figured he'd gone around the other way.

Eliminate the threats first.

She ran to the two guys she'd just shot. One lay on the ground. The other was still on his feet. The one with the *Rolling Stones* shirt. Older than the others.

He clutched at his arm. Tried to bring his gun up as Jade approached.

She darted left. He actually got a shot off. He staggered to his knees.

Jade raced in. Ripped the gun from him. She drove her elbow into his jaw. He stumbled away.

She went to the next guy. Took his gun. She saw the look of hate in his eyes.

Her shot had gone through his left shoulder. The arm lay like a deadweight on the ground.

He wasn't going anywhere.

With two loaded guns now, Jade grabbed the guy still on his feet. She pressed a gun barrel into his wound. "Tell your friend to come on out."

"He'll shoot you dead before he does that."

"What's your beef with me?"

"You shot us."

"Right. You started it."

"What is this?" He laughed. "The playground." He put on a whiny voice, "Oh, teacher, he started it."

"Funny." Jade shoved him away. She shot him in the calf.

As the guy fell, screaming.

Jade moved toward the trees. She desperately wanted to check on Sebastien. No way to do that with a fourth gun out there.

She didn't know where the last guy was.

The sound of the fire continued to grow. Heat rolled from the shack. Not that there really was any shack now. Just blackened timbers, mostly hidden by the flames and smoke.

"I know you're out there," Jade shouted. She started backing toward the trees. Her feet squelched on the damp pine needle layers.

She tucked one of the guns into her belt. The gun's barrel dug into her spine.

Jade kept backing up. She stole a glance toward Sebastien. She could just see him lying facedown in the grass.

He hadn't moved.

Cinder from the shack fire swirled into the sky. From far in the distance she heard a siren.

Jade could hear how the calls would have gone. *Gunshots fired*, and, *Fire! Fire!*

No sign of the other man. He had to be somewhere in behind the burning shack.

"Show yourself," Jade called. If he was over there he probably couldn't hear her over the fire. Jade could feel the heat from it even from fifty yards away.

She'd almost reached the trees now. Her boot kicked a pine cone. Needle-laden branches stretched overhead.

The three guys still lay on the ground. Bleeding. Groaning. Jade figured if the cops were coming, and the fire department, an ambulance would tag along.

She was a bit worried about the guy she'd shot in the thigh. Easy to bleed out from there. Especially if she'd hit an important artery.

But right now, she couldn't risk checking on him. That kind of thing got you shot.

But there was a way. If she backed on through the trees. Used them for cover. Sebastien lay just a few yards from the margin of the woods. Fifty, sixty yards to get around to him.

The sirens were closing in. They might be

minutes away. But in a situation like this, things changed in seconds.

As she moved back, she saw the fourth guy come around the blaze.

Carrying a bigger gun.

It looked–however outrageous that might seem–like an M16 machine gun.

CHAPTER NINE

From through the trees the sound of the sirens continued. Still too far away.

Too far away to make any difference when a guy with a machine gun stood only yards away.

The cabin raged. A column of thin smoke curled into the air.

And Jade froze.

The guy kept moving around the fire. He held the gun at almost shoulder height. Both hands on it. Ready to swing and shoot.

An M16 could do a lot of damage, Jade knew. A favored, basic gun for infantry. Few moving parts. Never jammed.

The guy didn't need to aim. General direction and an automatic burst would do the trick.

He hadn't seen her.

Wind blew the dying fire around. The shack creaked and cracked. Timbers fell from the roof.

The guy kept moving.

Around Jade, a cool wind blew in. Moving through the trees.

The guy stopped. Looked left and right.

Looked at his friends still writhing and groaning on the ground.

He started moving again.

Jade didn't trust her aim. Not with an unfamiliar pistol. Not at this range. Wind and the fire. It all made it hard to place an accurate shot.

The guy, on the other hand, had a machine gun.

Not an even fight at all.

Jade moved back. Slowly.

The shadows of the trees gave her the advantage. And her own dark clothing would hide her well.

As she stepped and set her foot down she heard the snap of a twig.

She stopped.

The guy hadn't heard. Too close to the noise of the fire.

Jade moved in behind a trunk. The bark was old and chunky. The trunk had to be over two feet in diameter. Enough to hide her.

She backed away a bit. Stood so she could just see the guy.

He moved the gun in a sweep around the trees. Satisfied, he ran to his fallen comrades.

Jade crouched. She checked the magazines in both guns. One full, one short by two bullets.

She clicked the magazines back in. Set the second gun back into her belt.

The flames were beginning to settle.

The guy with the machine gun slung it across his back. He crouched to the guy Jade figured was the boss. *Rolling Stones* tee shirt.

They spoke briefly.

The guy with the machine gun gave a nod. He stood.

He looked directly at Jade.

He started running.

Right for her.

CHAPTER TEN

The sounds of the sirens changed. They'd reached the rutted access road.

The fire would have the cabin in ruins in a few more minutes. Not much any fire appliance could do about that. Maybe keep the woods from going up too.

The guy lifted the gun as he sprinted. The fire behind turned him into a silhouette.

The gun's strap buckle clicked against the barrel.

She dove to the right. Landed on a pine cone. It dug painfully into her side.

She barely noticed.

The guy started firing.

Too high. The bullets hit trunks or branches. Or whizzed overhead into the woods.

Jade lay on her stomach. She took aim.
Fired.
Three shots.

The third smashed his hip. He fell like a building coming down from demolition charges. The machine gun spun away.

The leader swore. Shouting and cursing. Promising Jade all kinds of painful deaths. Mingled with that came epithets about the intelligence of the guy with the machine gun.

Jade stood. She walked to the one she'd just shot. He lay on his side in the crushed grass. He'd smeared some mud on his face when he'd landed. Like the others, he writhed and moaned. Smooth skin. Barely even shaving.

She pushed him over onto his back. He screamed.

"You'll be okay," she said.

Standing, she scanned the area. Didn't look like any more threats. She trotted by the others, hurrying to Sebastien. Past the bathtub. She saw rust spots inside where the enamel had chipped.

Sebastien had a wound right in the back of his head. His hair lay matted and sticky with black blood. Plastered to his scalp.

Not much blood. He'd died instantly.

Jade didn't even need to check his vitals. They'd killed him.

The sound of the sirens increased. Almost here.

Jade turned to the fire. All of Sebastien's research. Gone.

She bet that he didn't have copies. Didn't have anything online. It would all have been inside the shack.

What had he done to raise these people's ire? Looking into his uncle's disappearance. Rich

Cooper.

Why didn't they want Sebastien to know about it? He must have been close. Very close.

Jade choked for a moment, her throat clenching.

They'd come here because of her. *Heard you might have gotten some help.*

The guy had meant Jade.

We'd like to discourage that.

'Discourage' seemed like too light a word for what had just transpired. Four wounded. One dead.

Sure was some kind of discouragement all right.

Jade took a breath. She needed to ask some questions.

"I'm sorry Sebastien," she whispered. "We'll get to the bottom of this. Promise you."

She turned away and walked back to the ringleader. His breathing came in gasps. He clutched at his wounded arm. Blood leaked through between his fingers.

"You threw those Molotovs?" she said, standing over him, gun held loosely. Aimed vaguely at his midriff.

He told her to go somewhere unpleasant.

"Charming," she said. Through the trees she could see red and blue flashing lights. The cops.

Jade looked at the gun in her hand. Probably the one that this guy had used to shoot Sebastien.

Now covered in her fingerprints. And shells from it had shot the fourth guy.

Not a good look. Not if the cops found her

with it. That would take some explaining.

Of course ballistics and timelines would come into it. The gun would still have some of the wounded guy's prints. Probably, though, it wouldn't have any provenance. He wouldn't show up on records as the owner.

It wasn't as if they'd set out to frame her for Sebastien's murder.

But a less than thorough investigation might end up going with the easiest option. A lone person from out of state, versus a local, with witnesses.

Jade wouldn't stand a chance.

Jade moved away from the wounded guys. She headed around toward her Ram. The fire continued. Soon it would be nothing but embers and ash.

As well as the slashed tires, the Ram now had blistered paint across the hood and along the front fender.

With a crunch of gravel, the cop car pulled up. Another one came in behind. One was a county police department Caprice. The other a sheriff's department Seville. Blurred jurisdiction. Or just the sheriff happening to be in the area.

Jade crouched and put both guns on the ground. She headed toward the cops.

"Got four wounded," she called as the county guys got out of their car. A man in his fifties with a thick gray mustache and a slight paunch. In a trim uniform. Gun holster. Nightstick at his belt.

The other, the driver, was a woman in her early twenties. She came out of the car with her hand on her holstered pistol.

"Stay where you are," the woman told Jade.

"Easy, Sandy," the man said. "Let's get the lay of the land first off."

Jade guided them to the wounded quartet. Together with the sheriffs, they got started on first aid. An ambulance and a fire appliance arrived.

The paramedics took over from the cops, and the fire fighters doused the already diminishing blaze.

Jade talked with the middle-aged cop. Officer Derek Milton. She told him how things had happened. His younger offsider pulled on gloves and bagged up the two guns.

More cops arrived. Another ambulance. A young paramedic checked Jade for injuries and burns. Aside from a bruise where she'd landed on the pine cone, she was in good shape.

"You came through that pretty well, I'd say," Officer Milton told Jade.

"Looks that way. I guess there's a whole lot of history here."

Milton shrugged. He had a unique way of doing it. Noncommittal, but as if he knew something. "I probably shouldn't talk to you about that. You're a material witness now. I don't think I need to book you just yet, but I need to take you back downtown to get your statement."

The fire was about out now. The fire fighters working to damp down cinders in the foundations. A single jutting blackened piece of framing timber was all that was left of the shack that was still upright.

"Downtown?" Jade said.

"Figure of speech." Milton scratched at his mustache. "I just mean back to the station. Pretty small department really." Milton looked around the cars and cops. "Looks to me like everyone on the force is here right now."

"Okay." Jade glanced over at the Ram. "I suppose my truck's part of the evidence chain too?"

"Yes. This whole area's cordoned now. Forensics will have to go over the whole place with tweezers, I imagine. I think they'll have to send someone up from out of county. Haven't had that happen since the Chappin shooting back when I was a rookie."

"Couple of years ago then?"

Milton smiled. "Charm me all you like, I've still got to take you downtown."

Sandy, his young partner came over from helping the paramedics. She sighed. "This is what we call a complete mess. Excuse my language."

Milton leaned toward Jade. "Sandy's a Baptist. I have to put up with that kind of language all day long."

"I'm almost offended," Jade said.

Sandy gave a vague smile. "Let's take her back downtown." Sandy glanced toward the others. "The sheriffs are talking about making an arrest."

"They are? Me?"

A nod. "I told them to talk to the captain. It's our jurisdiction. They don't think so."

"Well, you would know." Milton leaned toward Jade again. "Sandy's fresh out of college. So all of that jurisdiction and Miranda and proper firearm protocols stuff is still right there in her frontal lobe." He tapped his forehead.

"You bet it is," Sandy said. "And I also know when to beat a hasty retreat."

"That you do." Milton turned to their Caprice. He opened the back door. "If you would," he said to Jade.

She nodded. Taking a last look around the carnage and destruction, Jade got into the cruiser's back seat. She looked over toward Sebastien.

Paramedics had covered him with a white tarp. Jade felt a pang. He'd come to her for help. Look what it had cost him.

This was going to take a whole lot of digging. What had Rich Cooper been tangled up in that his nephew found himself murdered a year later?

Jade knew she could leave now. Once she'd given her statement, these cops weren't going to hold her. They might ask her not to leave the state, but then, they might not.

She wouldn't be leaving anyway.

She needed to figure out who these guys were.

CHAPTER ELEVEN

Ivan Mortowitz stared at his face in the bathroom mirror.

Jacobsen's Interiors had redone the second floor bathroom a year ago, with a new shower and a fancy double basin and vanity. As if he and Rosemarie would brush their teeth at the same time.

He had to hand it to his wife, she sure had an imagination.

From outside came the cawing of a crow. The sound carried from the yard to the second floor. A number of the crows had taken to bothering other birds around a feeding table Rosemarie had installed under the old sycamore.

One of the things with having an estate was that anytime you tried something new, or improved something, it seemed to create a whole other problem. Feed the sparrows and jays and attract a murder. Mortowitz smiled at his own pun.

But the crow problem reminded him of this whole Rich Cooper deal. Or mess.

He rubbed his chin. In the mirror he saw his grizzled and lined visage. He looked older than his forty-eight years. More gray in the beard now than black.

"Still handsome, though," he murmured.

Mortowitz shaved quickly.

He would have liked to have had a rifle range on the property. Somewhere he could release some tension with a good rifle. They had the space.

He was a good shot, even if he liked to leave the strong-arming to others. Arm's length was always good.

But county ordinances were what they were.

Couldn't go disturbing the neighbors who lived a half a mile away.

Still, he got out to *Beckman's Rod and Rifle* often enough. A hundred rounds into the targets. Kept his tension down. And his eye in.

As he stepped back to the bedroom–similarly imaginatively decorated with a zebra-print quilt on the bed and a painting of a glittering outer banks sunrise hanging on the wall behind–his cell began ringing.

That would be Doug Maeberry. Reporting back on the morning's activities.

Maeberry, like his boys, was an idiot. Chumps, the lot of them. But they kept him at arm's length and usually got the job done. Sometimes that simply involved picking up someone from a pier and delivering them to an airport, other times it involved strong-arming.

Mortowitz picked up the slim phone from the bedside table. He saw Rosemarie's discarded clothes lying on the bed. She would be out for a run with friends. Tennis later.

The phone's screen told him *unknown number*.

Mortowitz smiled. Most of his calls came in like that. People he dealt with liked to remain anonymous.

He tapped to connect.

"Are you alone?" the voice on the other end said. Male. Hint of a northern accent. Maybe even Canadian.

"Who is this?" Mortowitz did not like demands.

No answer. Mortowitz heard nasal breathing. Another sound in the background. Maybe a dog barking.

The breathing continued. Clearly no answer was coming.

He reached to the drawer in the bedside table and took out the little Smith and Wesson revolver he kept there. A durable, reliable six-shooter. He'd had the ivory handle custom made in Jacksonville. He liked the weight of the gun in his hand.

"I'm alone," Mortowitz said, turning to face the window.

"You're going to want to get down to see the little fiasco outside of Fernville City. If you were, and I'm betting you would be, interested in containment."

"Containment?"

The line went dead.

Mortowitz looked at the screen. He tapped in to dial back the last number, but the screen came up with *number withheld*.

Well, isn't that something? Mortowitz stared at the screen.

He would have to talk to Sandy Kendel. She would be able give him the inside scoop on that.

CHAPTER TWELVE

Jade sat in the beat-up office chair and picked up receiver on the old desk phone. The police had let her use the phone in a vacant office in back of the station. The room had clearly been repurposed for storage. Cardboard filing boxes lined one wall. Old printers and phones stacked on shelves.

Boxes with defunct printers and phones stood on the desk. A tiny space barely large enough for the phone and a legal pad held on against the encroaching stacks.

Jammed in the corner were a couple of other office chairs in even worse shape. Both missing wheels and screws and with torn upholstery. They smelled of damp foam. The whole room smelled stale.

Jade dialed and waited. Angus Webber rarely took more than a few rings to answer. He kept his phone permanently diverted. She heard the clicks of the system, then he answered.

"Jade?" he said. "I saw something on the net about a fire down near where you were headed."

"News travels fast." Jade gave him a rundown on events. Webber found her work. Mentored her. Always had good advice.

"So you're at a police station now?" he said when she finished. "On the Outer Banks?"

The window looked out on the same woods. A robin stood on a pine branch. The bird stared back at Jade, twittering.

"Right here outside of Fernville City." Jade looked the other way. Internal windows faced the busy main office. Milton sat at a computer typing in his report. Sandy stood talking with another officer. A reporter had come in and was asking questions of the desk clerk.

"Fernville? Well, at least it's a city. There's that."

"No. It's a county." Jade sipped at the coffee Sandy had brought her. Strong and bitter. Just the way Jade liked it.

Outside the police building, Jade had seen when they'd brought her in, lay a small town square. Oaks and plane trees. A war memorial of sorts. A few park benches. The county court building, and the chamber of commerce, both facing into the square too. Some nice cars parked out front. A pair of shiny, dark blue Chevy Impalas. Next year's model. Quite different to the popular black pickups.

"A county." Angus sounded nonplussed.

He would. Last Jade had heard Angus Webber had headed into Chicago and almost settled down. An inner city apartment in a high rise. One of the places that allowed the owners to purchase neighboring apartments and knock down walls to expand their living space. Jade figured Angus would have taken three. Maybe even a whole floor.

He liked cities.

Angus had been one of her main contacts these last five years of freelancing. Without her own home base, she needed someone to find her work. As often as not that involved hunting down untouchable crime lords and unfindable high-level escapees. Murderers, embezzlers and rapists all.

She'd been surprised how much money the official channels of the system could funnel into such off-the-books enterprises.

Official agencies liked results. And none of them could pursue things in quite the way she could.

Suited her just fine. Her particular skills, acquired from years of training, both physical and mental, lent themselves to exactly the kinds of jobs Angus and the others—Blake Cotterill and the even more mysterious Kilross—came up with.

"It's a nice little place," Jade told Angus. "Tasty diner on the highway, wildlife in the woods." As she looked, the robin took to the air, vanishing over the building.

"I suppose if you like that kind of thing."

"So happens that I do."

"So you're in the right spot. But, I guess that's enough with the pleasantries. I'm sorry about Sebastien. He seemed like a nice enough kid."

Jade knew that Sebastien wouldn't have gone directly to Angus, but the contact would have come through a series of intermediaries. Someone who knew someone who knew someone–who knew how many times?–who knew a contact who once had dealings with someone who knew Angus.

It might have even come through from that lousy investigator. Or more likely his clerk Maisie Souther. They felt like Jade's second port of call.

The first being the three guys now under police guard at the hospital, and the other in a cell in another part of the building.

"They shot him dead," Jade said. She could still see him collapsing in her mind. "All because I came to help."

"You feeling guilty?"

"I'm not *that* Catholic. But yes, I'm feeling guilty."

"Wasn't your fault."

"But I was a trigger. There might have been some other trigger some other time, but the point is that it didn't take much to push them. Sebastien was onto something."

"And the fire then?"

"Consumed everything. All his notes. Pictures. Maps. Gone."

"So these people knew what they were doing?"

"I think so. Just looking for an excuse."

"From the tone of your voice I'm guessing you're thinking that they found the wrong excuse."

"They sure did."

"Did I remind you that there's no money in this?" Angus sounded weary.

"I think you did." Jade glanced up at a knock at the door.

Milton. He pushed the door open a fraction. "Did you want a coffee? I can... oh." He spotted the coffee on the desk.

"I won't be long," Jade said.

Milton gave her a smile. "I wasn't trying to hurry you." He glanced back out to the main room and back at her. "Captain would like to ask you some questions, though. Take your time."

Jade took a sip from the coffee. Getting a bit cold now. "Another five minutes. I can call again later."

"Sure. Fine." Milton scratched his mustache and made a little wave. He stepped back. The door clicked shut behind him.

"So," Angus said. "He didn't ask why you didn't have a cell phone. I guess cell service hasn't reached that far yet."

"You make it sound like I'm on the moon."

"Might as well be."

Jade gave a quiet snort. She always traveled light. At most she carried an ATM card and a couple of hundred in cash. Mostly she could find somewhere to get online and move cash around. And despite the ubiquity of cell coverage, she could always find a payphone. Or someone willing to lend her a couple of minutes on their phone.

Or, as here, an office with landline phones.

"What's your next step?" Angus said. "I've got other jobs lined up here. A young man in Mexico who thinks he's the next drug lord. A smuggling ring running who-knows-what across the Canadian border right there into Montana. Some guy on Long Island who's busting chops and selling tainted coke. That one should interest you."

"It does."

"There's money in it. And chances are we can grease some more palms to track your father."

Jade sighed. The reason behind all this.

Gone for more than two decades. Where was the man? She'd needed answers since she'd been a kid.

She knew it was an obsession now. She had to see it through. And these jobs paid for it. The man was proving to be the hardest one of all to track.

"Except for one thing," she said.

"I know what that is," Angus said.

"You do?"

"Yes. You feel like you owe Sebastien."

Jade didn't need to answer. Angus knew her too well.

She filled him in on everything she knew so far. It turned out that she hadn't uncovered much more than ?

Sebastien–through several intermediaries–had come to Angus. Sebastien's Uncle Rich Cooper had vanished a year ago. The family didn't know what had happened.

When she was through, Angus said, "So what's your next step?"

What was her next step? A visit to the bar where Rich Cooper had last been seen. A talk with Maisie Souther and her investigator employer. Even if just to find out his name. Tracking down more of Sebastien and Rich's relatives.

But one thing seemed obvious ahead of all that.

Talking to the guys who'd burned Sebastien's shack.

"Think that's such a good idea?" Angus said.

"Yes I do."

Milton knocked on the door again. "Sorry, sorry," he said. "The captain's getting impatient now."

"I'll be right there." To the phone she said, "Angus, I'll call you again later."

"I won't be home, but you can try."

"Okay." She hung up and stood, turning to Milton. "Let's go see your captain."

CHAPTER THIRTEEN

The captain's office was warm, and the window looked out over a picnic table set in a square of lawn cut into the trees. One of the officers sat at the table eating a sandwich and drinking from a water bottle.

The plaque on the captain's desk read Jonathan K. Bainer. A pleasant enough early middle-aged man with photos of his kids and wife on the tidy desk.

"Bess, Grady and Athena," Bainer said, seeing Jade looking at the photo. "Bess chose the names."

"You don't have to explain. They look like nice kids."

"Yes they are. That was taken about five years back. Grady's out of high school now. His band's trying to make it in Nashville, go figure. Athena's talking about pre-med. So much for me retiring early."

Bainer's fingers clicked on the mouse as he went through his notes on a computer screen. "Looks all in order. I don't think we need to hold you." He frowned. "Your address," he said. "'Care of'. What's that?"

"I don't have a residence at the moment."

A deeper frown.

"I travel," Jade said. "A lot. Easier to sell-up than have all those mortgage and utilities and taxes to deal with." A kind of truth. Jade had never gotten around to owning her own place.

"Taxes, I know it." With a faint smile, Bainer looked over from the screen. "All right. I guess Officer Milton suggested you don't leave the state? I'd like to make that formal." The captain met her eyes. "Don't leave the state."

"I won't," Jade said.

"I'm sorry about your friend. Sebastien."

Jade nodded. "Thanks." As she stood, she heard a shout from in the main office. Immediately followed by something crashing to the floor.

"Stay here," the captain said, darting around the desk.

Jade followed him through the door.

The main office area was almost empty. Most of the cops were all busy elsewhere.

Milton stood across the far side. In a doorway. Coffee in one hand. Other hand on his pistol.

The desk clerk stood with his hands raised. A plastic rack lay on the floor behind him. Brochures about reporting crime and traffic safety scattered around.

A young woman stood just across the desk

from him. Blonde, bad skin. Angry.

Behind her stood a gangly teenage boy in a ripped tee shirt. He faced out the main entry doors.

A shotgun in his hand.

Keeping a lookout.

"Katie!" Captain Bainer called. "Why don't you go on home?" He stepped slowly over, hands raised too.

"You got my brother here," Katie said. "Come to take him home."

The tip of the black barrel of a shotgun rose just above the counter level

"You can't do this Katie. If you don't go home now, how am I going to explain it to your parole officer?"

"Don't care. You people shot him. All he was doing was driving. Driving out there."

"I know. It was an accident." Bainer kept up his slow walk. "Lot of confusion. Someone burned down Sebastien's shack. A car got damaged. We're still trying to figure out who was where and who did what."

"Think I care? Joe's blood. Sebastien's a Cooper."

Jade felt her anger rise and it surprised her. How could this woman be so annoyed about the kid in the cell? Sebastien was dead.

"Katie." Bainer almost reached the counter now. "You can't come breaking people out of jail. It doesn't work like that. Put the gun down."

Katie stared at him. "You let me see him? He should be in the hospital with the others. You know that? Not in some stinking cell."

"I know, but they didn't have the beds, Katie. And he's not hurt bad. A flesh wound."

"Not what I hear. I hear he was screaming."

"He wasn't screaming. He held it together. I had to put him somewhere. And he's been away before, remember. It's for his own safety, you know that. I've got to follow procedure."

Katie sighed. She lifted the gun and lay it on the counter with a clunk.

Jade felt tension drain from her.

"Wasn't loaded anyway," Katie said. "And I've got a license to carry."

"A handgun, Katie. Your license is for a handgun." Bainer put one hand on the desk clerk's shoulder and the other on the gun.

Bainer lifted the gun and broke it open. He put it on the floor.

"You want to come see him?" he said.

Katie nodded. "I can get my gun back later?"

"Sure. That's fine. But I don't want you toting it around town, okay?"

"Okay. Come one Eddie, let's go see your brother."

The teenage kid–singularly focused on his guard duty until that moment–turned to face the room.

His eyes met Jade's.

"She the one who shot them all up?"

"What?" Bainer said. Jade realized Bainer hadn't seen Eddie's gun.

Eddie shifted the weapon. "Karl talked to Murray. Murray said it was a tiny little woman who done all the shooting."

Bainer glanced at Jade.
She stayed right where she was.
Eddie lifted his shotgun.
Aimed it right at her.

CHAPTER FOURTEEN

From outside the police building came the sound of a truck engine braking. Just for a moment. The sound faded.

Inside, the coffee pot bubbled. There were no other sounds. As if everyone inside was holding their breath.

Eddie looked around, wide-eyed.

"Eddie?" Jade said. "Is that your name?"

The kid squinted at her. "I could just give her a flesh wound too," he said. "How about that Katie? Even the score?"

"Eddie," Katie said. "Captain Bainer's going to let us go see Joe. No sense in getting yourself locked up too now."

"She done it." Eddie took a step toward Jade. "Tell me you didn't do it, huh? Tell me you didn't shoot them all."

"Eddie. Put the gun down."

"It's what you came here to do." Eddie glanced

at Katie. Locked his eyes back on Jade's. "Came her to fix this."

"We did. Now you're making it worse."

Jade admired Katie in that moment. She'd gone from aggressor to negotiator in a flash. Anger drained.

Eddie took another step.

"How," he said, voice distant and measured, "could it be worse?"

Eddie sighted along the shotgun's barrel.

"Eddie," Bainer said. "You can't give anyone a flesh wound with a shotgun. You know that."

Eddie took another step. Only five yards from Jade now.

"Maybe," he said. "And maybe I don't want to just give her a flesh wound. She shot four people."

"Eddie," Katie said. "She could have killed them. She didn't. She winged 'em all. They'll be fine."

"She can't aim, is all."

Another step closer. Three yards from Jade. She could see beads of perspiration on his forehead.

"And let me tell you," Eddie went on, "I sure can aim. I can aim real good."

Almost close enough that Jade knew she could disarm him. Duck. Dive. Grab the gun.

The kid could probably aim just fine out the back of their property with a line of tin cans on a fallen log. A whole different scenario here.

Of course, he didn't have to aim at all. Close enough now with the shotgun that he could do some serious damage.

Which was why she didn't duck and grab the gun. Too many other people around who could get hurt.

"Eddie please," Katie said. "You don't want to go away like your brothers. Like me."

Eddie swallowed. Jade kept facing him. She kept her expression blank. Anything she did could provoke him. Katie was doing the best job of talking him down.

"Doesn't matter," Eddie said.

Another step.

"It does matter. Eddie. Put the gun down."

"Gonna happen someday anyway. These guys are gonna book me for something. Might as well be something I actually done. Murder. Huh! That's top of the pile isn't it?"

"Eddie please."

He pressed the gun right into Jade's face. Inches away.

CHAPTER FIFTEEN

From the corner of her eye, Jade saw Katie shift. Closer to the main desk. Jade lifted her hand. Hoped Katie took it as a message to stay put.

The cold tip of the gun's muzzle looked like an open mouth on an angry feral animal. A badger ready to snap.

Inches from her face.

Jade could smell the gunpowder from the gun's use.

"Eddie," Katie said. "Eddie. Calm down. We've worked this out."

A sound from outside the police building. A car pulling up.

On a nearby shelf the coffee machine beeped.

Eddie's hands had the slightest tremor. The open end vibrated right in front of Jade's eyes.

He stared right at her.

Scared. Angry. A mess of teenage emotions

swirled in his eyes.

"Eddie," Jade said quietly.

He bit his upper lip. Made an odd sucking sound. Stiffened.

Kept the gun right on her.

"You got a girlfriend, Eddie?"

He blinked. "What? You applying for the job?"

Jade gave the slightest shake of her head. She was aware of the silence around her now.

She could see through the glass doors. The driver getting out of the vehicle that had just pulled up.

Coming toward the entry.

"Eddie," Jade said. "I was just wondering what your girlfriend would think of you shooting me."

"Proud. She'd be proud. Being a man. Standing up for the others."

"Nope. She'll be sad, for a while."

Another blink.

Outside, the driver kept walking. He couldn't see what was going on inside the building.

The moment he pushed through the doors he would know.

Because Eddie's reflexes would take over.

He'd pull the trigger.

"Sad," Jade said. "Because yours isn't the only gun in the room."

Blink.

"And if you shoot me, then the cops are going to shoot you."

The driver was only a few yards from the doors.

"And then your girlfriend will come to your funeral. After that, she'll probably hook up with that other guy. Craig? Brad?" Jade had no idea, but there were always other guys hanging around.

Eddie swallowed.

"Harlan," Katie said. "He's got his eye on Trudi. Always has."

Eddie sucked in a breath. "She never would."

The driver reached for the stainless steel door handle.

"Eddie," Jade said. "This your last–"

She jerked her right hand up. Shoved the barrel.

The blast tore a hole in the ceiling. Made her ears ring.

Jade kicked Eddie in the gut.

He went down. Let go of the gun.

Jade held it up. Broke open the breech. Dropped out both shells.

Milton and Bainer moved with precision. The held Eddie down. Cuffed him.

Katie started crying.

The driver outside had retreated to his vehicle. It started and drove off.

The pair of cops hauled Eddie to his feet. Milton looked at Jade.

"Some morning," he said.

"Not even lunch time."

"It will be soon," Bainer said gaze fixed on Jade. "And we're taking you to lunch. You've got a whole lot of explaining to do."

CHAPTER SIXTEEN

The diner looked pleasantly normal after everything. A regular big-windowed, highway eatery. Big sign over the door. The friendly smells of home cooking drifting from inside.

Jade headed inside, with Milton and Bainer right behind.

"Hello there," Chakana said as Jade walked inside with the two cops.

"Guess you liked the cook up this morning." Chakana's beaming smile lit up the crowded diner.

"Got to get some more," Jade said. "Recommended you to a couple of friends."

"Welcome," Chakana said to Milton and Bainer. "Don't see you two in here often enough."

"Hi Chakana," Milton said. "How's that ratbag boyfriend of yours?"

"Ah," Chakana said with a wave of her hand. "He's gone roughnecking out in the gulf. I told him about that film about the rig that caught on fire, and he told me how much they were going to pay him. Then he sent me a break-up text. I called him so many names. Can I find you a table? We're pretty busy right now, but I've got a booth coming free in a couple of minutes. Just got to clear those dishes."

Sure enough, a couple of minutes later Chakana had the table ready. Jade sat with the two cops. Around them families and couples sat eating a variety of meals. The smells of the food wafted in a pleasant, appetite-inducing swirl.

"You all take your time," Chakana said, handing them menus. "I'll go grab you some napkins."

"Ready," Bainer said without looking at the menu. "BLT. Coffee and a bearclaw."

"Likewise," Milton said.

Chakana grinned. "That leaves you, Honey."

"BLT," Jade said, returning the smile. "Coffee. Bearclaw."

"Well aren't you all just the easiest table? You bring these guys back anytime." Chakana headed away out to the kitchen.

"Maeberry family," Jade said to the two cops.

They looked at each other.

"Actually," Bainer said. "I wanted to ask you where you learned to negotiate. You did well."

"I was thinking that about you. You talked Katie down."

Bainer shook his head. "I know Katie. Deal with her a whole lot. She was just a bit upset."

"She brought a shotgun."

Bainer nodded. "Sure. Thing was I didn't

notice Eddie. Not really. He's a kid. He's been in the background, but not really a part of what the rest of the family gets up to."

"Picked him up for shoplifting a couple of times last year," Milton said. "Cans of soda from the gas station. Not exactly leading to what happened today."

"Trying too hard to follow the family tradition?" Jade said.

"Looks that way," Bainer said. "I dropped the ball there. I don't know how I can apologize for that. If you'd played it any differently... well."

"It might have gone badly."

A nod from Bainer.

Chakana arrived with the coffee jug. She filled everyone's cups. "This is not bottomless," she told Bainer and Milton. "Three cup maximum."

"That's not a rule," Milton said with a smile. "You made that up just now."

"Doesn't matter when I made it up, it's still a rule." Chakana headed along to the next table.

Jade sipped from her coffee. As before, it was strong and bitter. "So this family," she said. "Known troublemakers."

"That they are." Bainer took a good swallow from his coffee. "Try to stay under the radar, but they're not too... well." Bainer tapped his temple with his index finger.

"Too good at forward planning you mean?" Jade glanced around the diner again. People quietly eating. Families and truckers. All basically oblivious to the events of earlier.

Milton laughed. "Polite way of putting it."

"So what's going on with what happened out

at Sebastien's shack?" Jade felt that twinge in her heart again. Sebastien dead. All his research burned. For what?

And why?

"How do you mean?" Bainer said.

"I mean…" Jade trailed off as Chakana arrived, arms laden with their BLTs. One plate on each hand, and the third balanced on one forearm.

The sandwiches were huge. Thick-sliced home-baked crusty white bread, stuffed with lettuce and tomato and long strips of glistening bacon hanging out. A wooden skewer held the top slice and filling in place. A pickle, some grapes and a big dollop of Thousand Island dressing lay on what little space remained at the side of each plate.

"Delicious as always," Milton said.

Chakana set their plates down. "Back in a sec' with those bearclaws."

Jade took a bite from her sandwich and it really was delicious. She swallowed and said, "I might have to move down here."

"At least then," Bainer said, "you'd have a place of residence."

"Funny," Jade said and took another bite.

"Maeberry family," Milton said, setting his sandwich down after two bites. "They'll do anything for a dollar."

"Arson?" Jade said. "Murder?"

Milton glanced at Bainer, who took a big bite from his sandwich. He pointed at his mouth as he chewed.

"It doesn't quite add up, does it?" Jade said. "Doug Maeberry. The older guy."

"You shot him a couple of times," Milton said.

"Yeah. He'd already shot Sebastien. And he was going to shoot me. Maeberry called out, 'heard you might have gotten some help'. Meaning me. Then, 'we'd like to discourage that'."

"I read your statement," Bainer said. "That's word for word how you gave it."

"I try to remember like that. Better that way. What is their interest in Rich Cooper? And what was Sebastien closing in on with his research?"

"That's the question." Bainer put his sandwich down. He told Jade how Sebastien had come by the police building every month or two asking some new question. Usually something simple like how jurisdiction worked for missing persons cases worked, or if it was possible for a private citizen to get a subpoena for information another private citizen held.

"He spent hours at the library," Milton said. "He knew the answers, just wanted confirmation really."

"Verged on obsessive," Bainer said.

Jade nodded. She'd seen that on his wall in the shack. "His uncle went missing."

"Yes. It was news. Statewide for a day or two. Faded as these things do. We helped with support for the official investigation. Not enough leads. Didn't go anywhere. I believe the case remains open. Not our jurisdiction. Cooper didn't live in the county, and *Bernie's Rest*, the bar where he was last seen, is up in Talbert County."

"Can you get at the files?"

"Me?" Bainer seemed surprised.

"Here's what I'm thinking," Jade said. "The Mayberry family are a distraction. I'm surmising this is out of their league. Their attack on Sebastien wasn't personal. It was a job."

"Who for?" Bainer said.

"That's what intend to find out."

CHAPTER SEVENTEEN

Doug Maeberry lay staring at the hospital ceiling when Jade came into the ward. The smell of disinfectant pervaded the space.

The county medical center did a little bit of everything. From regular doctor appointments through to visiting specialists. The hospital wing out back boasted six beds and some surprisingly modern medical machinery.

The two others, Bud Maeberry and Ealing Cooper lay in the two other occupied beds. Both of the men were unconscious. Jade would have started with Ealing Cooper. After all, he was family.

"What do you want?" Doug Maeberry said as Jade walked to him. One arm had a drip. His other arm had a handcuff at the wrist, binding him to the bed.

The cop at the door to the ward kept a weary eye on them as he flicked through a magazine.

Jade guessed he'd spent the last couple of hours flicking.

"Who are you working for?" Jade asked Maeberry.

"I work for myself. Why don't you get out? We'll see you in court when they charge you with shooting us."

"Yeah. Looks to me like that might go the way of self-defense. So that won't be why you find yourself in court."

"Well I suppose we'll see you elsewhere."

Jade sighed. She pulled up the bedside chair. "You killed Sebastien. Given your reputation around here, I suppose that's not unusual. But what I can't figure out is why. What was he to you?"

Maeberry opened his mouth to reply, but Jade held her hand up.

"Just wait," she said. "I'll give you a chance. It strikes me that he was nothing. He didn't get in your way. Didn't do anything to especially annoy you. What I figure is that you and your boys have become dupes. Someone paid you to come around and harass Sebastien. More than once."

Maeberry licked his lips. He glanced at a glass half-filled with orange juice standing on the bedside rack.

Jade picked up the glass and passed it to him. Maeberry drank. He handed the empty glass back. It clunked as Jade put it back on the rack.

"You wanted Sebastien to stop looking in his uncle's disappearance."

Maeberry looked away.

"But what does it matter? To you, I mean."

Maeberry frowned. "You're no cop."

"No. I was helping Sebastien out. Trying to find his uncle."

"Rich Cooper." Maeberry nodded at Ealing, lying still unconscious in the other bed. "Ealing's uncle too."

Now Jade felt like she was making progress. Maybe it was the simple act of handing Doug Maeberry the glass of juice.

"So where does Ealing fit into this? He's not looking for his uncle the way Sebastien was."

"No one looked for Rich that way. Sebastien was insane."

"You knew him?"

Maeberry shrugged. He winced.

"Have you got pain relief?" Jade said.

A shake of the head. "Don't need it."

"You were shot. And, sorry for that. But surely you could get something?"

"You're not really sorry. I would have done the same. Worse, maybe."

"You didn't know Sebastien, but you knew what he was doing."

"That's right."

"But, to be honest, you didn't care. Rich Cooper's been missing for a year. You didn't even know him. Am I right?"

Maeberry didn't say a thing.

"But someone around here doesn't want anything more uncovered. Someone who might have paid you and the boys to, say, rough-up Sebastien."

Still nothing from Maeberry.

"So here's the thing," Jade said. "Chances are

there'll be charges laid against the three of you."

"Your prints are on the gun."

"Yes they are. Yet it seems that common sense will prevail. The three of you are handcuffed and under guard. It didn't take the cops much to figure out the sequence of events."

"We've been in trouble before."

"Follows your family around a bit, doesn't it?"

A nod. And then an admission that surprised Jade. "It does," Maeberry said. "But maybe we let it follow us too easy. Sometimes if the kids slowed down things might not go so bad."

"Who's looking for Rich Cooper?"

Nothing.

Jade stood. One of the others stirred in the bed. The handcuffs jangled on the aluminum rail. The cop looked up. Closed the magazine.

As Jade walked around the end of Maeberry's bed, she heard him whisper. Just audible.

It sounded like, "Ivan Mortowitz."

Jade looked back at Maeberry. "What was that?" Jade said. "A name."

Maeberry looked her dead in the eyes. "I didn't say a thing."

CHAPTER EIGHTEEN

Derek Milton drove Jade to the rental agency in Fernville City where she'd rented the Ram. He didn't talk all the way. Seagulls kited over the road. Traffic seemed to stroll along in a steady flow. Cars, pickups. Delivery trucks. An occasional bigger car or pickup towing a boat on a trailer.

The agency operated out of a little sky-blue prefab building with a gravel lot and Hurricane fencing. Situated right at the mainland shore, by the main bridge to Tollis Island. The young clerk had a gold piercing in her eyebrow.

A half hour later, and a lot of explaining and calls back to the captain at the police department, Jade had another truck. A Ford F-150 in silver. New, but with a couple of dings. Far too powerful for what she needed, but the only thing they had on the lot aside from a couple of Kias and a Malibu.

"Not my style," Jade told the wide-eyed young clerk.

While the paperwork finally printed, Milton asked Jade about her visit with Maeberry.

"You get anything?" he asked.

"You took your time to ask."

"Musing over it. Kind of unusual to have a witness go talk with an accused like that. I'm surprised the captain allowed it."

"I talked to the right people. Technically we made it that I'm working with an on-going investigation and that Maeberry had pertinent information."

Milton nodded. "Like Captain Bainer deputized you."

Jade shrugged. "Not formally, but he gave me some leeway. I need answers."

"Rich Cooper."

"That's right."

"And with what happened, it honors Sebastien's memory to have the trail pursued."

"Thanks. I thought that too."

"So. Did you get anything from Maeberry?"

Jade shook her head.

"Really? You seem like the kind of person who could get anyone to talk."

"How about this? He didn't say anything admissible."

Milton pursed his lips and nodded. "We already got his statement. It will go to trial. Seems to me it's just waiting for the ink to dry on the charges."

"Yes."

"So whatever he said that wasn't admissible,

that might help your investigation?"

A thump on the rental agency's counter. "Sorry, excuse me," the clerk said. She rubbed her eyebrow. "Need for you to sign here, here and here. And initial here and here."

Jade signed and initialed and took the keys. "Thank you."

The clerk smiled. "Four slashed tires and blistered paint. The boss says this one better come back in better shape."

"Do my best," Jade said.

CHAPTER NINETEEN

Out front of the agency Jade fanned her face in the warm air. A semi trundled by. A big splash of advertising on the side announced the health benefits of California raisins. The truck sped away east, across the bridge.

Jade and Milton walked around into the rental agency's yard, boots crunching on the gravel.

There were only two vehicles in the yard. A little red Kia and the F-150. Milton laughed. "I can't picture you in that baby car."

"Hey, nothing wrong with a Kia."

"I know. I'm not sure about the Ford either. Not like you've got anything to prove."

Jade smiled at him. "I feel like I've always got something to prove."

Milton scratched his mustache. He glanced around, looking toward the bridge. Overhead a gull squawked. "So," Milton said. "I was thinking, maybe you could use some help?"

"Help?"

"I'm offering. I know I'm older, but I'm still ambitious. I'm planning taking the detective exam next year. Lot of study. Jumping in on your investigation here would be good for me."

Jade stared into his eyes. She noticed how green they were. With a mischievous twinkle.

"Don't you have a job?" she said, looking him up and down. "I see you in this uniform. You were at the office and, oh yes, were the first at the crime scene." Jade was trying to make light of it all. Sad, though, all that had happened. Sebastien. Had it just been this morning that she'd been having breakfast with Sebastien?

"Ah, the uniform," Milton said. "I'll go get changed. I already okayed it with Captain Bainer."

"But haven't you got this big investigation going on now anyway?"

"The state and the sheriffs are taking that over. And I've got fifty days leave owing. More or less."

"So the captain is giving you time off and you're going to hang with me kind of doing police work? There's a name for people who do that."

"Chump?"

Jade laughed. "I know a guy from England who talks about busman's holidays. You know, where a bus driver…"

"I get it." Milton sighed. "I suppose you're the kind of person who likes to work alone anyway?"

"Kind of. But I always appreciate good company."

"I can be good company. Some days."

Jade jingled the keys. "It'd be good to bounce ideas off someone else too."

"I can bounce ideas." Milton glanced at the police cruiser still parked out front of the agency.

"I'll follow you back," Jade said. "You can drop your car off. I guess we can swing by your place so's you can get changed."

"Deal, then." Milton said, holding out his right hand.

Jade took his hand and they shook.

"Deal," she said.

CHAPTER TWENTY

Milton's house was a clapboard bungalow set in scrubby pines along a narrow tarmac strip. All the homes on the street–lane, really–had big properties. The nearest neighboring house lay over a hundred yards off.

The land around the trees lay covered in brown needles. Jade saw a pair of squirrels speeding up one of the trunks, making a helix path. One of the squirrels stopped and peered over as Jade pulled up at the curb.

A ten-year-old BMW stood parked in Milton's driveway. Jade opened the rental's door and stepped out. The squirrel remembered it was busy chasing the other one and raced on up the pine trunk.

"Come on in," Milton said. "You can tell me your plans for the next step while I get changed."

"Ew, no."

"From the living room, sheesh." Milton

sighed. "That's me, always tongue-tied around the ladies."

"Did you just call me a 'lady'?"

"I'm very traditional."

"Sure you are. It's your partner who's the Baptist."

Inside, the house was immaculate. The kitchen bench was clean and empty. A rack of three jars on the shelf above neatly ordered and labeled. *Coffee, Sugar, Tea, Cocoa.*

The living room carpet looked recently shampooed. Jade sat in one of the armchairs facing the television.

"Maeberry gave me a lead," Jade called.

"He did?" Milton called back from the bedroom. His voice echoed through the house.

"Ivan Mortowitz. Does the name mean anything to you?"

"Haven't heard it. We could check the police database. And others."

"Good. Second thing I want to do is go visit the bar."

"The bar?" Something thumped. Jade guessed it was Milton putting on his shoes.

"*Bernie's Rest*," she said. "That's where Rich Cooper was last seen."

"Good place to start then." Milton appeared in the living room doorway wearing fawn Dockers, a plaid shirt, a Red Sox baseball cap and Caterpillar boots. He looked down at his feet. "I know, I know."

"What?"

"I need to work on my style."

"That's a style."

"Funny. Sandy says I just need a woman around the place. You know so I don't–" Milton imitated Sandy's voice "–*Go out looking like that.*"

"You look fine," Jade said. "Ready to get to work."

"That's what I tell her." His eyes widened. "Sorry, I just realized. I didn't mean anything by that. You know, like... that you..."

Jade smiled at his tongue-tied attempt to extricate himself. But she said, "That's fine. I didn't think you were. Not averse to the idea, but I'm working."

"'Not averse', well, that's something I can tuck away for my ego."

"I didn't mean it like..." Now it was Jade's turn to feel tongue-tied. He was an attractive man, if at least fifteen years her senior. Professional and intelligent.

It had been a long time since she'd had a fling.

Milton grinned. "Well, let's go on with this investigation and we could see where that leaves us."

Jade nodded. "We could. Yes." She felt a tingle up her spine. Anticipation. A long time since she'd felt that too.

Perhaps it would be good to team up and see what happened. Might be good to even think about a home base too. North Carolina was as good as anywhere.

Milton stood looking at her for a moment. Jade looked back, feeling the smile grow on her face.

A solid knock on the door broke their reverie.

"Visitor," Milton said. He headed back to the hallway.

Jade stood. She saw Milton had some silvery trophies on the mantle. Baseball and golf. Some of them for participation, others for most improved player. One for most home runs in a season.

She heard Milton talking with someone at the door. Female. Jade couldn't make out their words, but it sounded like Sandy, Milton's partner.

Jade headed toward the hallway. Was Sandy going to offer to help too? An interesting thought after the tenor of Jade and Milton's conversation moments ago.

The presence of a third person would certainly temper any libidos.

Jade stepped into the hallway. Right away she saw something was wrong.

Sandy had her gun in her hand.

Held almost casually.

Milton had his hands raised. Just above waist height. Not in surrender.

More like he was trying to calm her down. Sandy was in her uniform. Still at work.

Sandy's eyes fixed on Jade's.

"Knew she'd be here," Sandy said. With a lurch, she pushed past Milton.

Darted into the hallway.

The gun came up.

Sandy started shooting.

CHAPTER TWENTY ONE

Wind blew through the hallway.

Joined by the *thwack, thwack, thwack* of bullets striking the wall.

She ducked back.

Through the door.

Into the kitchen. She stumbled. Rolled. Came to her feet. Right by the refrigerator.

The shooting had stopped. Sandy swore.

She burst into the kitchen.

Jade yanked open the fridge door.

It smacked into Sandy. Milk and soda tumbled out. The soda can exploded. It shot across the floor on a trail of bubbles.

Sandy fired again. Right into the door.

The door blasted back at Jade.

The refrigerator shook. Bottles clinked.

Jade felt a stinging pain in her knee. She

staggered back. Banged her head against the bench.

The bullet had gone through the door. Hit her knee.

Jade scrambled to her feet.

"They said you were a fast one." Sandy had the gun aimed at Jade's face. "Told me you could turn the tables quick. Looks like they were half right."

"Who?" Jade said. "Who told you?"

Sandy glanced away at a sound from the hallway. She moved around so she could cover both Jade and the door. Milton came through.

Only a few seconds had passed since Sandy had started shooting. She must have knocked Milton down in her rush through the front door.

"What's going on Sandy?" Milton said. He had his gun out now. Aimed right at Sandy.

Sandy kept her eyes and the gun on Jade.

Sandy blinked.

"You misjudged, didn't you?" Jade said. "You thought this would be an easy thing to pull off."

"You're smarter than this Sandy," Milton said. "What's going on in your head?"

Sandy didn't respond.

"Put the gun down." Milton kept his gun leveled at her. Jade could see hesitation in his eyes.

His partner. Instead of standing by him in an investigation, now holding a gun.

"Standoff," Sandy said. "And you don't even know the half of it."

"What don't I know?"

Sandy just shook her head.

"Ivan Mortowitz?" Milton said.

Sandy's eyes widened as she glanced at him.

Jade moved.

She kicked off the bench cupboards. Drove in low.

Tackled Sandy at the waist.

Sandy yelped. She smacked the gun down against Jade's back.

Jade winced. She kept moving.

Together the pair staggered along. Sandy tripped. Went down.

They slammed against the floor. Sandy coughed.

Even underneath, Sandy kept pounding at Jade's back. Sandy brought her knee up. Hard. Right into Jade's crotch.

Jade hung on.

Something hauled them around. Bone snapped. Loud.

Sandy screamed. She kept struggling, but the fight had gone out of her.

"I've got the gun," Milton said.

Sandy kicked out. Jade pushed away.

She lay panting. Wincing from lancing spasms in her back.

"Got her," Milton said. "I've got her."

Jade stared at the ceiling. She heard the jangle of handcuffs. The clicks of them locking.

She breathed hard. Almost winded.

"You're creating a world of trouble for yourself, you know that?" Sandy said.

"Oh, shut up!" Milton said. "I'm going to gag you too."

CHAPTER TWENTY TWO

Milton's house felt cool. The wind gusted. A curtain in the kitchen fluttered. It reminded Jade of a sailboat.

More peaceful times.

Cars pulled up outside. Jade knew there would be neighbors gathered around their own kitchen tables. She wondered how often they heard gunfire like that.

Milton stood leaning against the kitchen doorframe. He stared at the holes in his fridge door. Jade leaned on the bench. It was all waiting now.

"I guess," Milton said to Captain Bainer when he arrived with three other officers, "that you're cancelling my leave now?"

"Well, heck no," Bainer said. "If you weren't already on leave I'd make you take some."

A lone burger wrapper flipped and tumbled along the street, carried by an increasing wind. Standing on Milton's front steps, Jade listened to a dog barking from somewhere nearby.

The other cops had already loaded Sandy into the back of their cruiser. She sat glaring back at Jade.

"Quite a day, huh?" Milton said.

"You could say that. And I need for both of you to drop by and give statements." Bainer looked over at Jade. "That'll be your second one today."

Jade nodded. Her back twinged even from that small movement. "Do you know her connection to all of this?"

Sandy had three broken fingers from when Milton ripped the gun from her hand. The other cops seemed as surprised as Jade at Sandy's actions.

"It will come to light." Bainer shook his head. "So much promise you know."

"I know," Milton said. "I've been her partner for the last five months. On the job training. She always seemed more straight-up than anyone. Never let me get away with shortcuts on the paperwork or scuffs on my shoes."

"Exactly," Bainer said. "So. I'm getting back now. Lot to do. Lot of things to cover." He looked back and forth between them. "You know if it wasn't you, I wouldn't be letting you head off on your own. I'd bring you in now. For your own protection."

"I appreciate that." Milton gave the slightest of smiles.

Shaking his head, Bainer stepped away and

headed along the front walk. The dog's owner hollered at it and the barking stopped. The burger wrapper got itself caught up on a shrub.

Bainer stopped at the car. He put his hand on the door edge and looked back.

"Someone tried to kill you," he said.

"No," Jade said, without shouting, but loud enough for him to hear. "She wasn't really trying. She went about it all wrong. A dozen other ways she could have approached it."

Bainer shook his head. "I said 'tried'. Tried and messed up. So, you be careful. Whatever you've uncovered it's meant to stay hidden. I need you to stay in touch with me. Let me know everything you find. Every step you take, you report in to me. Okay?"

Jade didn't respond.

"I've got your cell number," Milton said. "We'll report in."

"Good. Be careful." Bainer got into the car. The engine started and the vehicle pulled away from the rough shoulder. A moment later the car made a U-turn and headed back into two.

The second car stayed parked. The other cops doing crime-scene work inside, photographing and retrieving bullets from the ceiling and fridge door.

"So," Milton said to Jade. "Do you think that was friendly advice, or is my captain tangled up in all this too?"

"Your captain?" Could Bainer be tangled up in it all? First a cop shoots at her, then the senior officer tells her that whatever she'd uncovered *was meant to stay hidden.*

"I can see what you're thinking."

Jade nodded. "Yeah. I'm thinking we need to try something different. Off-grid and out-of-state."

"Right. But out-of-state is not possible."

"No it's not."

"So tell me the next move."

"The next move is a visit to our new favorite bar."

CHAPTER TWENTY THREE

Mortowitz drove his Mercedes along the rough driveway through the pines. The stink of fire smoke had pervaded the car's interior and he ran the aircon to clear the air.

Still stunned by what he'd seen. Police tape sectioning off the area around the blackened timbers that had once been a shack. Cops in white protective coveralls picked over the ground. Black Suburbans parked in a row along the shoulder. As little shoulder as the dirt track possessed.

What a thing.

Sebastien out of the way.

And the Maeberry clan in a world of trouble.

What ne needed was to get on home and sit and talk with Rosemarie. Clear his head of all this with something banal.

His cell rang. Mortowitz pulled it from his jacket pocket and tapped to answer.

"Mortowitz," he said.

"Yup." The same male, possibly Canadian, voice from earlier.

"Going to tell tell me who you are?"

"Strange that you don't remember me. I've even done a couple of jobs for you."

"Lot of people work for me."

The man laughed. "Sure do. Not that your tax returns would show any of that."

"Are you threatening me?" Mortowitz saw something move off in the woods to the right. Perhaps a deer. Yes. Standing in the pines. Glossy brown eyes staring at him as he drove by.

"On the contrary, Mr Mortowitz, I'm trying to help you out. Help you get ahead of this."

"I am…" Annoyed, Mortowitz cleared his throat. "I am getting ahead of this. Well ahead."

"You know that little errand you sent Officer Sandy Kendel off to perform?"

"How do you know all this?"

"My business to know all this."

"I'm really not taking a liking to you, you know that? You know what happens to people in that position?"

"And now you're threatening me."

Mortowitz didn't say anything.

"I think," the man on the phone said, "that despite having Sandy in your back pocket over that business of her brother, she's still got a soft spot for her partner."

Mortowitz kept driving. Phone pressed to his ear. Still didn't say anything. Ahead he could see the main road. A red sports car swept by.

"She's in custody," the voice said. Not Canadian, but definitely out of state. "And her boss is not happy at all. Probably she'll be charged with attempted murder. That's some hold you have over her."

Mortowitz took a breath. So that had gone wrong too.

"I suspect that woman who came out to give Sebastien a helping hand is not to be underestimated. I would say, 'proceed with caution'. No easy kill."

Mortowitz realized he did know who was on the end of the call. "Gary Petronas," Mortowitz said. "You're that investigator."

"Bingo," Petronas said.

CHAPTER TWENTY FOUR

It took Jade and Milton fifteen minutes to reach *Bernie's Rest*. Right out near the water. Jade drove in from the south. Along the island The Atlantic lay broad and rough to their right. Spray followed the whitecaps. Sand blew in wisps across the tarmac.

To their left lay the southern end of Glass Bay. The contrast between the bodies of water could barely have been more extreme. Glass Bay lived up to its name.

The bar stood on a section of the sand island raised and protected by an old concrete wall. The highway inclined up, rising perhaps four feet to the protected area. A few houses and other businesses stood in the area too, all looking tired and seaworn.

Jade parked the Ford out front of the bar.

Right next to a black pick-up identical to the one the gang had driven to Sebastien's shack.

"There are a lot of them around," Milton said, before Jade even mentioned the pick-up.

"I'm sure." The slight queasy feeling in the pit of Jade's stomach surprised her. Remembering Sebastien crumpling into the grass.

Jade and Milton got out. The sea breeze carried a scent of salt and gulls. The air was much cooler than back in Fernville City.

The faded and peeling sign announced *Bernie's Rest*. Small light fittings pointed at the sign. The building looked as if it had been repainted every year for the last fifty, and with all the cracks and chips, it looked like it could use another paintjob.

The door creaked as Jade and Milton stepped through. Dim lighting revealed some pool tables, a long bar, and some booths with threadbare upholstery.

From a jukebox along the side wall came the strains of a Rolling Stones classic. *Brown Sugar*. Jade smiled, amused at herself recognizing the track.

A woman stood at the bar, taking glasses from a cardboard box and placing them on the shelves beneath. A lone man leant over one of the pool tables, cue in hand, taking aim at the white.

"Officer Derek Milton," the woman at the bar said, pushing the box aside. "Not often we see you up this way."

"Claire," Milton said. "Nice to see you too."

The pool balls clacked. The guy made a whispered curse.

"You've missed the lunchtime rush," Claire said as Milton and Jade came up to the bar, "and you're just ahead of the evening crowd."

Milton glanced around. "Good to know that business is going well."

"Honey, I'm hanging by a thread here. If it weren't for Gus over there, I wouldn't be making any money at all."

Gus at the pool table glanced their way and grunted. He took another shot.

"Sorry," Jade said, "we're not big spenders."

"Two club sodas," Milton said.

"Seriously?" Claire rolled her eyes.

"We tip well, though," Jade said.

"Well, ain't that something?" Claire took a plastic bottle from the glass-fronted fridge behind and filled two tumblers with club soda. "Two fifty."

Jade slid across a ten. "Don't worry about change."

"I'm not a charity," Claire said, but she put the money in the till.

"We've got some questions about Rich Cooper," Milton said.

Claire sighed. "You know, my father started this place. Couple of years before I was born. He would tell me the stories. Three tough years as he got the place going, and learned how to run a business without bleeding cash nonstop. After that, fifteen good years. A couple of *great* years. And then the storms started getting more frequent."

Jade picked up one of the glasses and drank. The club soda was crisp and refreshing.

"Our location here was good," Claire said. "The old seawall protected the building, and the family home. Thing was that not everyone had that.

"Every year more people moved away. California, you know. You still have the ocean, but it doesn't swamp your house and strip the land."

Claire looked at the box of glasses and back at Jade and Milton. "Sorry, I get on a pedestal. I guess what I meant to get to was that Rich Cooper disappearing was frankly good for business. For about a week. The cops came by with questions. Ordered fries and coffee. Rubberneckers wondered what was going on and dropped in for a beer and a chewing of the fat."

"I know you answered a lot of questions back then, but Emily's got a few more."

"Jade," Jade said. "No one calls me Emily."

"I can't add anything to what I already told the cops." Claire looked Milton up and down. "I just realized, you're out of uniform. Have you lost some weight?"

Milton gave a nod. "Watching what I eat, training more often."

"Good for you."

"What I was thinking," Milton said, "is that maybe something's come to light since they first spoke with you. Which would have been almost a year back."

"Come to light." Claire pursed her lips. "Now that you mention it... nope. Rich came in here maybe three times a month. Kind of irregular regular if you know what I mean.

"That night I served him a couple of highball vodka with a twists. One for him. One for Jodie Clemons. A more regular regular. They'd dated for a while."

"Is she still around?" Jade said.

Claire nodded. "She lives up on Gatehill Plantation. Last I heard, anyway."

"She doesn't come in much anymore?"

"Oh sure. She comes in plenty. But she's kept it pretty close to her chest for the last while. Doesn't have too many friends here these days. We talk a bit. Sports, what we're planning to wear on the beach this summer, which highschooler's gone and gotten herself pregnant. Usual stuff. Nothing significant."

"You sound like a couple of men," Milton said.

"Hey!" Claire scowled at him. "When did you get all sexist like that?"

"Couple of weeks back." Milton just took it in his stride. Jade could tell he was good with people. Wouldn't he be wasted as a detective? Regular patrol seemed to suit his personality.

But then, detective work took a lot of those kinds of skills too. As he was displaying right now.

Milton looked over at Gus. "He a regular too? Did he know Rich?"

"Nope," Gus said. He took another shot. Sank the black. He walked around the table and dropped another four quarters into the slots. When he pulled the lever all the balls rattled and thumped through the channels and into the slot. He began setting the balls on the table.

"Big Ed was here that night," Claire said. "He

died four months back."

"Ed Hurlehy," Milton said. "I remember him."

The balls on the pool table made a sudden loud series of clacks and bumps. Gus, breaking.

"You want to have an investigation," Gus said, "you should go look into that."

"Gus," Claire said.

"Why do you think that?" Milton said. He picked up his club soda and walked over to Gus. Milton put the glass down on one of the nearby tables and fished in his pocket for some change. He put four quarters on the pool table's rim.

Gus concentrated on his aim along the pool cue. He took the shot, sinking one of the balls. As the white spun back across the table, Gus stood and looked right at Milton.

"They said it was accidental drowning. And that's how it stayed."

"You think otherwise?"

Gus's upper lip shifted as he used his tongue to rub his front teeth. He looked over the table. Bent and stretched, taking aim again.

"Big Ed was murdered." Gus jerked the cue. The balls clacked and another disappeared into the corner pocket.

Gus stood again. "Murdered plain and simple."

CHAPTER TWENTY FIVE

A cool wind blew onshore. Sand spackled the cracked concrete on the parking lot side of *Bernie's Rest*. A gull stood on the corner of the building's roof, watching Jade as she stepped out.

Jade had talked with Claire a while. Same details. Rich Cooper disappeared. Who knew where?

Jade walked back around *Bernie's Rest*. The building was in even worse condition on the seaward side. What little paint there was had faded to a bland pink-beige. The exposed boards looked gray and petrified.

Joining the building and the seawall, a wooden deck ten feet across held a couple of picnic tables. A heavy wooden door led directly into the back of the bar. In the middle of the door hung a brass doorknocker in the shape of sailing ship. A barque.

It looked like a long time since anyone come through the door to sit on the picnic tables. The tabletops had ancient ring-shaped stains.

A twisted wooden rail stood directly above the seawall, with one gap. Wooden steps led down to the saturated sand. Jade leant against the rail.

Gingerly at first, but she could feel that, despite its appearance, it was solid. Out between the breakers a gull sped, gliding fast through the troughs.

"Hello there," Milton said, coming around the side of the building to join her.

"How did your game go?" Jade looked up at high clouds. It would be sunset soon.

"Gus whupped me. I think I sank one ball, and that probably because he took pity on me."

"He does seem to spend his days practicing."

"Yeah." Milton leaned on the rail next to her. "Next stop?"

"I don't know yet. I'm starting to get a sense of why Sebastien needed his pinboard wall. There are a whole lot of elements to this."

"And now this new element. Gus is certain that Big Ed's drowning was nothing like accidental. He won't make a statement. Won't even say why. He doesn't look scared, but I think that's it."

"Gus doesn't seem like the kind of guy to give a whole lot away. I saw two facial expressions. Blank, and concentrating."

"Yeah."

Jade turned and looked at the building. She

pointed. That's the back of the men's bathroom there."

"Buoys," Milton said.

"Yes. Ha, ha. See how tiny that window is?"

"Sure. So?"

"So, Rich Cooper, according to Claire went into the bathroom and never came out. At least not back into the bar. So he came out through the window."

"Why?"

"How is my first question. I don't think Rich Cooper was a small guy. How did he get that high, and through that gap? And then down on this side."

The window from the men's bathroom was a foot-high, two-foot wide rectangle. The top of the frame nested in against the ceiling. The lower edge had to be over seven feet from the floor.

No doubt Rich could have reached the lower sill. Getting out out would have been another matter.

"Claire doesn't know how he got out," Milton said. "I already asked her that. The window frame only opens a few inches."

Rich Cooper would have had to push through without any leverage.

Perhaps desperation had forced his hand.

"I read the reports I could get hold of about it. Most of it's locked up in police files, but there are some elements there. There was some in newspaper files."

"But Sebastien had a whole lot more, didn't he?"

"Yes. I figured that I would look over what he

had and we would put something together."

"Because you're quite the investigator? You'd do better than the police, and the private investigator." Milton scratched his mustache, thinking. "Gary Petronas."

"Sebastien didn't get a chance to tell me the name before he was killed. But I would have tracked him down."

"Still can. I can look over the police files too. See if there's something that's not out in the media. Could be–"

"Hey," a voice said.

Jade looked over to see Gus coming around the side of the building. He still had his pool cue with him. Carried lightly at his side.

"Hi Gus," Jade said.

"So, I got call," Gus said. He stopped at one of the picnic tables and leant the pool cue up against it. "And then a message confirm it."

He stopped. Standing between them and the path around the side of the building. He pulled out a cell phone.

Jade checked the distance from where she was to the steps down to the beach. She figured that the back door with the brass knocker was locked or jammed.

There was no space to get around the other side of the building. A fence separated the deck from the next property, butting right up against the back of the bar.

She realized she'd gone on the defensive automatically. Checking out escape routes. She didn't even know what Gus's call meant.

"A call," she said. "About... Rich Cooper?"

"Kind of." Gus glanced at the cell phone. He tapped at the screen a couple of times. "Here. This is the message; 'Don't let them leave'."

"Meaning us?" Jade said.

"That's right."

"Who's it from?"

"Unknown number."

"But you spoke to them first? You recognized the voice?"

"Yeah, I did."

"So?" Milton said. "Who was it?"

"Gary Petronas."

"The investigator?" Jade said.

"So I heard."

"Intriguing," Milton said. "I guess we shouldn't leave. See how it plays out."

CHAPTER TWENTY SIX

As the sun set, Jade and Milton sat in a booth near the front of the bar. Claire brought them burgers from the grill as she dealt with the evening crowd. The jukebox played a John Denver standard.

More of a bar than a restaurant, *Bernie's Rest*, did offer a small menu. As well as burgers, there were hotdogs, nachos and 'tater skins'.

"You know what I like about this place?" Milton said. "Windows. So many bars are dank and closeted and Bernie had the foresight to put in some windows."

It still felt dank and closeted to Jade. The windows–four of them–were barely bigger than dinner trays. They looked right out into the parking lot.

The evening crowd consisted of a pair of elderly men, Gus at the pool table, and a couple of local guys who'd arrived in yet another black pick-up.

Jade picked up the burger, surprised by how hungry she'd become. The burger was huge, and pieces of beetroot and tomato fell out onto the plate.

"How can you eat?" Milton said.

"Hungry," she said.

"No. I get that. I mean, with not knowing what's going on around us."

"Gary Petronas?" It was unnerving, Jade admitted to herself. The man had wanted Gus to make them wait. Perhaps he was coming to warn them off.

"Exactly," Milton said.

"You know him?"

"Local investigator, but you know that. I met him a couple of times, maybe. He's been into the police station to ask for some details about his own investigations."

"So he's all licensed and legit?"

"Yes. Ex-military, if I recall rightly. An MP down in Fort Sunderland in Georgia for at least a decade. Set himself up as a P.I. when he got out. I think he might have some money too. Inheritance or something, so he doesn't have to work. All this is hearsay, of course."

A silver ten-year-old Audi pulled up outside, parking in next to the second black pick-up. Out on the road, a big campervan drove by.

A tall man unfolded from the Audi. He wore jeans and a business shirt with a gray-fawn sports jacket. He waved at Jade and Milton as he approached the diner.

"So this will be Gary Petronas," Jade said.

"The one and only," Milton said. Now he picked up his own burger and started eating. Beetroot and tomato fell to the plate.

Petronas came through the door and made straight for them. The way he strode, and his height, made Jade almost surprised that he didn't wear a Stetson. He had a cowboy swagger about him.

"Howdy," she said when he reached the booth. "We're eating. Feel free to order something."

Petronas looked back at the bar. "Nah. I ate here once. Threw up all the next day." His accent had a soft lilt to it. Jade could picture him on the range in northern Montana.

"Sorry to hear that. But please sit." Jade scooched over in the booth.

"Well, I'm not eating, but I will grab a drink. What are you two having? You got coffee there? Little late in the day for coffees. Whyn't I get you something. Beer? Something stronger?"

"I'm good with coffee here," Milton said.

"I could go with a beer," Jade said, knowing she wouldn't drink it, but wanting to avoid alienating Petronas.

"Beer then." Petronas headed over to the bar.

"Why," Milton said, leaning over toward Jade, "do I get the feeling we're going to leave here with more questions than answers?"

Jade just raised her eyebrows at him and took another bite of her burger.

Petronas came back moments later with three bottles of Heineken in one hand, and a tumbler with ice and amber liquid in the other.

"Before you say anything," he said, sitting

down, "the other two beers are for me." The bottles and tumbler clinked on the table. "I'm one hundred and nine days unsober after three hundred and fifteen sober. I have decided to embrace my inner alcoholic with a focus on moderation over abstinence."

Jade saw Milton's eyebrows rise.

"Three drinks is moderation," Jade said.

"Well, three drinks to start." Petronas kept his eyes on Milton. "And, no, officer, I won't be driving. A DUI is inconvenient in my profession. To say the least. My secretary will be coming by to pick me up on her way home."

"Maisie Souther," Jade said.

Now Petronas raised his eyebrows. "You do your homework." He picked up the first of the beers and took a good chug.

"Of course," Jade said. "We needed to track you down."

A nod. "Shame about Sebastien. So, of course I'll do all I can to help you. Access to all my files on Rich Cooper. Anything else I can do." Petronas looked around the bar.

"So that's why you had Gus have us wait?"

"And," Milton said, "how did you know we were here?"

"This is a small community, officer."

"Right," Jade said. "So how does Rich Cooper go missing and no one knows how? And when Sebastien tries to find out, he's killed for his trouble."

Petronas licked his lips. He took another pull from the bottle. "You know, I think maybe I should grab a bite. Absorb some of the effects of the alcohol. You want me lucid here." He glanced toward the bar. "What do you recommend?"

"Nachos," Jade said, at the same moment as Milton said, "Hotdog."

Petronas grinned. "You're a right duo, aren't you?" He took a deep breath. "I know I'm taking a risk coming here. Those Maeberry folk aren't the only ones in Mortowitz's pocket."

"You know about—"

Petronas held his hand up. "Let me go order. All will be revealed momentarily."

He stood and headed for the bar.

Milton stared at Jade. "No wonder Sebastien did so much research on his own."

Jade took another bite of her burger, trying to enjoy it. At the bar, Petronas negotiated with Claire.

The two local guys sipped at beers. None of them looked around the bar at all. They didn't speak.

Gus continued playing on the pool table.

CHAPTER TWENTY SEVEN

The jukebox played on. Nothing on it, apparently, from this century.

Through a hole in the wall behind the bar, Claire worked in the bar's little kitchen. The balls on the pool table clacked and rumbled. Frequently one dropped into a pocket.

"Let me paint you a picture," Petronas said, beer in hand and waiting for his nachos to arrive.

Another car had pulled up in the lot, with a group of three guys in their twenties who could have been lumberjacks. Plaid shirts and hefty, scuffed workboots. Long beards on all of them. Thick arms and pumped chests. The group leaned on the bar and made eyes at Claire.

Jade kept an eye on the guys. Perhaps this was just that evening crowd building. A tingling sense told her it might be something else.

"Rich Cooper was entangled in some nasty stuff," Petronas said.

"Such as?" Milton took a sip from his coffee and a bite from his burger.

Petronas shrugged. He looked up as Claire brought over a big plate of nachos, steaming with chili and cheese. Jade kind of wished she'd ordered that.

"Trucking," Petronas said, picking up a chip. "Boating." He took a bite. Chewed. "Mmm, those are good." He picked up another chip.

"Trucking and boating," Milton said. "I'm not following you here."

Petronas smiled. Ate the chip. Swallowed. "Rich's Mom was over in Italy when he disappeared, you know that?"

"We know," Jade said. Sebastien had given her the precis of things back in the diner. It had turned out that Rich had booked a ticket for a flight to go and meet her there.

"Flying out the next day, or something," Petronas said.

"Not 'or something'," Jade said. "You should know the exact time and date."

"The next day, yes. Never made it to Charlotte for his connection. Never made it to Italy. Last time anyone saw him was when he headed into the bathroom right over there." Petronas pointed through the bar toward the back wall and the door marked 'buoys'."

"Was he fleeing?" Jade said.

"That could well have been the case. Only Rich knows that for sure."

"How did he get out the window?"

"I've asked that myself," Petronas said, taking another chip. "You go look at it. The window's high up. Narrow. How could anyone get through that? Maybe an eight-year-old kid. If someone gave them a boost. Not Rich Cooper, that's for sure."

Another pickup turned into the gradually-filling parking lot. This vehicle was red. Chipped and battered from long hard years.

A man in his thirties stepped out.

"I've had a thought," Jade said. "It's starting to get crowded here. Why don't we go somewhere quieter?"

"Quieter?" Petronas said, looking around. "The place is about empty."

"Filling up fast," Jade said, keeping her eyes fixed on Milton's.

"It is at that," Milton said.

Petronas looked at Jade. "You're not drinking your beer."

"What's your cell number?" Jade said. "Why don't you give me you give me your business card. We can set up a meeting for tomorrow?"

Petronas scowled. "See tomorrow I've got a meeting at a chicken farm. Down near Maple Hill. You need to move on this more quickly."

Petronas's eyes flicked toward the men at the bar. At the same time the new arrival came through the door.

None of the others looked around.

As if they knew he was coming.

"All right," Jade said. "We do." She picked up the beer and took a sip. "I'm going to use the bathroom." She shifted closer to Petronas.

"Sorry, we've been here a while."

"No problem." Petronas shifted out from the booth so she could stand. "I don't think this is going to take more than a half hour or so. You two are pretty deep into it already."

"We thought so." Jade took the bottle with her. As she made her way across the floor she could feel numerous eyes on her. The guys at the bar. The new arrivals.

Not Gus. Not the two elderly guys.

She felt like her suspicions were merited.

As Jade walked by the bar, Claire met her eyes. Claire gave a tight-lipped smile and a slight shake of her head. She followed along the bar to the end. Away from the other customers.

Jade slowed. Leaned in.

"Order a drink," Claire said.

Jade got it right away. She put the Heineken on the bar. "I could go for another one of these."

"Great. Won't be a moment."

Jade leant on the bar. A good opportunity to get the lay of the land here. Turning, she looked out toward the door.

Elderly men to her right, in another booth. Gus to her left at the pool table, still clacking balls into the pockets.

Three guys farther along the bar. The new arrival joined the other two at one of the standing tables.

Jade didn't see any weapons.

She turned at a clunk on the bar. Claire stood there with another Heineken. She took the nearly-full one away.

She leaned forward. Said, "Be careful."

Jade put a ten on the bar. "I guess these guys are not regulars?"

"I know them all. Never seen them in here before. They do their drinking at the *Crow's Nest.*"

"I'll watch myself."

"You should go. Now."

"Thanks for the advice." Jade picked up the bottle and headed for the bathroom.

As she reached the door, another two lumberjack guys came through.

Better odds now.

Jade braced herself.

CHAPTER TWENTY EIGHT

Mortowitz pulled up outside *Bernie's Rest*. He sat for a moment, enjoying the the thrum of the powerful engine under the hood of his Mercedes. The machine had been a good purchase.

The sun was already down. Which saved him from having to look at the ruin of a building in broad daylight. He could almost pretend that the place was a respectable bar.

Mortowitz shut off the engine and stepped out into the cooling air. He heard the cry of an evening gull. Even fifty yards away he could smell the beer and fries from the bar.

Not his kind of place at all. And the earthy types who dwelt here were not his kind of people.

In the scrappy, potholed parking lot outside the wreck of a bar, Mortowitz counted seven vehicles. A big Ford pickup, a little hatchback, several other pickups and Gary Petronas's Audi.

Mortowitz didn't have much regard for Petronas at all. Alcoholic. Moocher. Always looking for any angle he could use to leverage a little more cash from a job.

And the Audi was nothing but an affectation.

But Petronas had done one good thing here. Located that interfering woman. It would be useful to get all this wrapped up quickly and quietly.

Mortowitz took a breath and headed for the door.

CHAPTER TWENTY NINE

The 'Gulls' bathroom smelled clean and fresh. Clearly Claire took care of the place. Tired and worn, but clean at least.

Jade stared at herself in the mirror. She looked tired.

Some days went like this one.

She washed her hands and splashed refreshing cool water in her face. When she stood upright again she saw the door opening.

She picked up the Heineken bottle she'd set on the edge of the basin. She held the bottle by the neck.

One of the guys stepped into the bathroom. Big shoulders. Thick neck.

"Think you've got the wrong bathroom, buddy," Jade said.

The guy looked down at her. Smiled.

"Nah," he said. "I'm in the right place."

The guy probably had almost a foot in height on her. Maybe eighty pounds too. He might have been twenty years old. Probably worked out with weights three hours a day.

The kind of guy who'd probably won plenty of fights. Might have even won every fight he'd ever been in.

"You looking for me?" Jade said. "You don't need to send such a big guy. Someone could have just come to ask."

"Well, I'm here to ask." The guy put his hands together and cracked his knuckles.

"Ask what?"

"This." The guy lifted one tree-trunk arm. Drew it back.

Swung.

Jade was already gone.

The mammoth fist swept through clear air.

Ducking low, Jade knew she'd been right. A guy of his size was the wrong one to send. The confined space of the bathroom worked against his size.

He needed open space. In here there was no room for someone with his bulk to build any momentum.

Jade, on the other hand, had plenty of manoeuvrability.

She swung the bottle down. Right at his ankle.

The clunk was like an axe striking a tough old oak.

The guy howled. He jerked back.

Jade swung again.

Connected with his knee.

Another howl. The guy tilted. Staggered.

Jade grabbed his collar. Yanked him down. Used his weight to his disadvantage. Pulled him toward the basin.

His head made a nasty sounding crack when it hit the edge.

The guy collapsed. Just like Sebastien had. Into a boneless lump.

The door banged again. The guy's body blocked it.

"Busy in here," Jade said. "Give me a minute."

The door banged again.

"What's going on in there?" One of the other guys.

"Your friend's had a bad turn. I think you should go call an ambulance."

Another bang onthe door.

Jade patted down the prone guy. She came away with a folding blade and a small pistol. A Chinese weapon. The kind of thing with no history. Small and easy to carry. Probably took standard parabellum rounds too.

A quick click and Jade dropped out the magazine. 9mm parabellums all right.

The magazine slipped right back in. Clicked into place.

The door banged again.

"Almost ready," she said.

With a quick grab and pull she rolled the guy. Left a foot wide gap to the door.

She took the bottle in her left hand. Pistol in her right.

"All right," she said.

The door pushed open.

A head came through.

Jade swung the bottle up.

CHAPTER THIRTY

The bathroom made for very close-quarters fighting. A tight cramped space.

Better for someone little, like Jade.

Disadvantageous for someone big. Like the guy in front of her.

Like the other guys.

The bottle swept upward. Who might be coming through the door?

Jade's mind raced.

There were six more of them out there. None as big as this guy. But still big.

Could be Claire. Coming to see what the ruckus was. Though she would know. She'd already warned Jade.

Maybe Milton. He would have seen the guy come to the 'Gulls' door. Seen him go through.

Perhaps even Petronas. Unable to resist being an investigator and coming to investigate.

Chances were none of those.

If it was, she had a split second to pull her swing.

She didn't have to.

The head belonged to one of the lumberjack guys.

The bottle cracked on his nose.

The guy's head jerked back. He collapsed across the other guy's legs. Broken glass rained around him.

Jade spun. Straddled them both. Through the doorway she could see into the bar.

The other guys all on the move.

Jade grabbed the second guy's belt. She hauled him partway into the tiny bathroom.

His legs jammed up in the doorway. She couldn't get him far enough.

She glanced up.

Guns out. The other guys approaching.

Milton and Petronas on their feet. Claire standing right at the far end of the bar.

Jade couldn't see the elderly guys. But someone else came through the door. A businessman.

He gaped at the scene in front of him.

"Come out now," one of the guys said. Gun in both hands. Pointed right at Jade.

She grabbed the second guy's ankle. Jerked it up. Got him right through the door.

Jade dove to the floor.

She got her shoulders against the first guy's belly. Her feet against the wall under the basin.

She pushed. Hard.

Grunted with the effort. She managed to shift them though. Inch at a time. They slid back.

Slowly.

Pushing back against the door.

Someone outside shouted.

Incoherent.

Angry.

And then another voice. Angry.

But definitely coherent.

"Come out now. We will shoot."

They wouldn't. Not with their friends in the bathroom.

"Going to count to three."

Not with a cop out in the bar.

"One."

And witnesses.

"Two."

Jade lay right down. Pressed herself back into the bulk of the first guy.

"One."

CHAPTER THIRTY ONE

The big guy stank of beer and sweat. Jade's heart pounded.

The rough floor pressed into her.

The count had finished.

Nothing happened.

No shooting.

Starlight glinted through the high, narrow window louvres. Jade figured she should have gone out through that earlier. Just the way Rich Cooper had in the bathroom next door a year back.

"Count's done," the voice from out in the bar called. "Now we start shooting."

Jade had a gun herself now.

Useless in this situation. Unsighted. Innocent people out in the bar. Too risky.

The gunshot made her jump.

High. Through the door. The bullet hit the wall by the mirror. Lodged there for a second.

Fell.

The bullet tinged on the floor when it landed. A xylophone kind of sound.

The bullet rolled bumpily and came to a stop.

"You still alive in there?"

Jade smiled. It would be just plain stupid to reply.

But then, maybe that was what it would take. Call them out.

She had no strategy right now.

She jumped at another gunshot. The sound made her ears ring.

High. But not as high as the last one.

They knew their guys were down. The guys outside aiming above.

Risky too.

And now she had a strategy.

She looked up at the window. The sill was six feet from the floor. Easy enough to grab and pull up. Knock out the louvres.

Drop to the other side.

Three seconds.

A lot of bullets could come through that door in three seconds.

Whole magazines' worth.

Jade took the little pistol. Got a good grip.

"Still alive in there?" the voice shouted from outside.

Sounded close to the door.

Maybe even close enough to be hit.

Staying pressed in against the guy's deadweight, Jade moved her arm around. Forearm against his side.

She aimed up. Almost at the top of the door.

"You should come on out now." Very close to the door.

Jade fired.

Three shots. Through the top of the door.

It was a light door. Hollow core. Cheap. The kind of thing that a few good shoulder charges would break down.

The guys' bullets had come through barely slowing. *Knife through butter*.

Jade hoped hers went straight through too. Straight into the ceiling.

From outside came cursing. The sounds of furniture scraping. Bar stools falling to the floor.

She fired two more shots.

Counted three seconds. Fired three more.

More shouts from outside. Panic.

Good.

Jade rolled. Stayed pressed close to the first guy. She patted down the second guy.

Found his gun.

And another magazine.

He'd come prepared.

Same Chinese model. Same ammunition.

With the first gun, Jade fired again.

Lower.

Figuring everyone would be down on the ground by now.

She emptied the magazine.

Anyone out there would know that. Smart money put them at trained at least well enough to count.

Assuming any of them could count higher than ten. Or count at all.

She fired two more shots from the second gun.

Letting them know that she had more than one magazine to play with.

More than one gun.

One more shot.

Now she scrambled. Jumped for the window.

She used the gun's butt to smash the panes of the louvres. It sounded loud. Glass rained down. Inside and out. Smashed up more on the floor.

Jade dropped. Crouched. Fired again.

Two shots. High into the door.

More shouts from outside. Maybe she'd overplayed her hand.

She jumped for the sill again. Pulled herself up. She felt the pinpricks of broken glass jabbing her palms.

Scrabbling up she twisted through the open gap.

Another gunshot.

Instantaneous flaring pain in her calf.

They'd shot her.

CHAPTER THIRTY TWO

The narrow window frame scraped at Jade's legs. Some part of it jabbed her back. The sound of the ocean beyond the seawall seemed strangely calm.

People were shooting but the waves simply continued.

Jade slid forward. Awkward, but she got her legs through the gap. She dropped to the wooden deck.

Tumbled into a heap.

The air was cool. He leg thrummed. The pain was diminishing.

Leaning forward she checked the wound.

A scratch, really. Not a decent shot. And through the door. The bullet would have been deformed and spinning. Traveling fast, but the passage through the door had slowed the bullet enough that it struck her a glancing blow. Right in the meaty part of her calf.

The jagged wound was bleeding. She might even need some stitches.

But she was still mobile.

Getting to her feet, she tried the leg out. Took a few hobbling steps.

She wouldn't be running any marathons or sprint races anytime soon, but it would do. The leg throbbed.

Claire probably had a first aid kit inside the bar.

Jade almost laughed out loud. Getting inside the bar would be problematic at best.

In the darkness out in the ocean she saw the lights of a ship. Coastal traffic. Just below, she could see flecks of glistening white spume as the incoming tide lifted the height of the low breakers.

It would be a beautiful sight if not for the situation.

Jade kept moving around the building. All the vehicles were still in the parking lot. Pickups. Her Ford. Petronas's Audi. A Mercedes parked at the edge. All lit by one single high old sodium light at the road's edge.

Jade slowed. She looked around the building's corner.

She hated not knowing.

A gull squawked from a post across the road.

Jade took a step. Came up to the first of the small windows.

She peered in.

A shambles inside. Furniture overturned. People lying on the floor. No one upright.

Jade changed out the magazine on the empty

gun.

One full. One short by five.

But it meant she had a gun in each hand. She carried the full gun in her right hand.

Crouching, she hurried to the bar's main door.

From far off, the direction of Fernville City, she heard the sound of sirens.

Too late.

Jade stopped at the last window. She stood and peered in again. Chances were even if someone was looking out they wouldn't see her. Despite its dim lighting, the bar was still lighter than outdoors. Anyone looking would just see mostly reflection.

Now she saw more. One of the guys lying close to the bathroom door. Others down among the furniture.

Someone shouted something. Another one scrambled across to the 'Buoys' door. Sat with his back up against the wall.

Jade saw his mouth moving. Talking to the guy on the floor.

Someone else called. Jade caught the words this time.

"Kick open the door."

"Can't. She's blocked it."

"Then shoot her again."

Maybe thirty seconds had passed since she'd gone out the window.

Surely they should have guessed that.

Another guy scrabbled across. Sat in next to the first one. They had a whispered conversation.

Then, with a nod, they both swung around. They lay on their backs and scrabbled over in front of the 'Gulls' door. They pulled their legs back.

"What are you doing?" one of the others shouted.

They didn't answer. They just kicked at the door.

It shifted.

Opening a bit.

Both of them fired inside.

Jade moved to the bar's entry.

CHAPTER THIRTY THREE

Grit lay on the concrete path in front of the diner. Jade took careful steps. Wan light shone through the small windows.

Jade had a better feel for the lay of the land now.

Two guys unconscious in the 'Gulls' bathroom. Three guys right at the door.

One more, whose legs she could see sticking out from behind a cluster of fallen stools and tables.

That left two. And she didn't know where they were.

The sirens drew closer. Back along the shore, through the darkness, Jade could see distant flashes of blue and red light.

Another sound too. The crunch of shoes on gravel.

Then a car door opening.

She looked around. The cabin light in the Mercedes showed a head of dark hair.

The door clunked shut.

The car backed away. Stone chips spat out from under the tires. The vehicle skidded.

The driver looked right at Jade. Black eyes. Nondescript male. He spun the wheel.

The Mercedes sped forward. Hit the tarmac. Fishtailed. The tires squealed on the hardtop.

The car picked up speed. Vanished into the night.

At least someone got away from this mess. Jade hoped everyone else was okay.

She focused back on the door.

Shouting still came from within. Probably they'd discovered that she'd gone.

She pushed her way inside.

The door banged. The five guys at the bathroom were her lowest priority. Way down the list.

Openly visible and easy to keep an eye on.

It was the others she needed to worry about.

The one whose legs lay just visible by the overturned furniture.

And the other one. The one she couldn't see.

Hiding behind the furniture too probably.

Perhaps that was their play. Perhaps they were intentionally acting stupid. Playing at that they knew she was still in the bathroom. When in fact they knew she'd gotten out.

And right now the last guy had a bead on her. Could drop her at any time.

That they intended to kill her was obvious. No question.

She just had to meet that intention with an appropriate response.

The door creaked as she pushed it open.

Jade stepped through.

CHAPTER THIRTY FOUR

The jukebox continued to play. Something by Travis Tritt. Not as familiar as the Rolling Stones. A jaunty guitar strum, though, with laid-back drumming. Travis singing about lost loves.

The smell of beer had a faint overlay of cordite.

Too much shooting had happened.

Two of the guys by the bathrooms stared at her. Mouths open. Eyes wide.

They honestly thought she was still in there.

Less than a minute had passed since she'd exited. But clearly this operation had sent just the muscle. Left the brains behind.

Jade shot the exposed leg that stuck out from behind the fallen stools.

The guy screamed. The stools bounced aside as he clutched at his leg.

"Don't," Jade shouted as the guys at the bathroom started to get to their feet.

She kept the gun her left hand aimed at them. Enough bullets to disable them all.

She couldn't keep her focus on them. She needed to look around the room.

But she could keep one of the guns aimed at them. They might be bold enough to try something, but when you've got a gun pointed your way, discretion usually wins out.

Anyway, she'd already bamboozled them by escaping the bathroom.

The guy she'd just shot continued to moan.

Holding both arms out Jade kept her back to the entry. She scanned across the bar to her right. Moving her right arm with her focus.

She saw Petronas's feet sticking out from under the table. Shaking. Scared.

Keeping her left hand aimed at the three by the bathroom, Jade brought her right hand around. Both guns on them. The three guys continued to stare at her.

"Where are the others?" she said.

No response.

Jade scanned to the left, bringing her left hand around to cover the room.

The two elderly guys still sat at their table. As she came around, one of them picked up his beer and took a gulp. The other one gave Jade a nod.

She nodded back.

Jade scanned the room again to halfway. Still no sign of the missing pair.

"Milton?" she said. "How are you doing?"

No response.

Jade took another step. The sound of the sirens leapt. Not far away now.

"Petronas? How about you?" Jade was worried about Milton.

"Still alive." A tremble in the investigator's voice.

"You see where Milton got to?"

"Didn't see anything."

"Could use your help out here now."

A moment's silence. Petronas slid out from under the table. He sat and looked around.

"Do you see the other two?" Jade said.

"Other two?"

"Two more of these guys." Jade kept her gaze and the guns focused on the three at the bathroom door. None of them had moved an inch.

"I heard a gunshot," Petronas said. "I hit the deck. I'm no longer in the military."

"Yes. But you know how to handle a gun." She handed him the gun from her left hand, tucking her hand under her right arm as she maintained aim.

"I can keep them covered," Petronas said. "If that's what you mean."

"That's what I mean."

"Got it." Petronas took the gun in both hands. He held it rigid and out ahead. Finger with a millimeter gap to the trigger.

Jade went toward the bar. She checked the guy she'd shot.

"You good?" she said, hand on his shoulder. She kept the pistol close and obvious. Pointed at his shoulder.

The guy swore at her. Called her something filthy.

Jade smiled. "You're okay then. Keep that hand on the wound. It will minimize the bleeding."

He grunted.

Jade moved around. Closer to the bar.

Able to scan from a different point now, she looked back.

And saw Milton.

Lying under another one of the booth. One back from where they'd been.

Odd. There seemed to be someone there with him.

Struggling.

Right away Jade understood what she was looking at.

Milton and one of the guys. Wrestling.

As Jade took her first running step, she heard another sound.

Claire.

From the bar.

A squeak. A quiet 'help'.

Jade turned.

The last guy had her by the neck. A wicked smile on his face.

And a pistol pressed to Claire's temple.

CHAPTER THIRTY FIVE

The damp bartop glistened. As if Claire had just finished wiping it down. As if everything was ordinary.

As if some thug didn't have her by the neck.

"What do you want?" Jade asked the guy.

He kept the gun pressed into Claire's temple. She gave a whimper.

The jukebox made a quiet click. Travis Tritt was done with his sad story. The opening tones of a Randy Newman song began.

This one was probably just as sad.

"Tell him to put the gun down," the guy holding Claire said. He nodded toward Petronas. "Nice and easy."

"I'll do it," Petronas said. He tipped his hand, raising the gun, and began to crouch.

"Wait," Jade said. "Petronas, keep them covered."

"Not smart, lady," the guy behind the bar said.

Over Randy Travis's ballad, Jade could hear two things. The first was the noise of Milton struggling with the other guy.

The second was scream of the approaching sirens. Almost at the bar.

"The way I see it," Jade said, staring right into the guy's eyes.

He kept the gun pressed to Claire's head.

"You can end up killing more people here and do thirty to life in Leavenworth." Jade glanced at the gun in her hand. "Or you can take your chances with the cops."

She could shoot him. If she wanted. Jade knew she was a good shot. But she hadn't fired this particular gun except for just now. And it was a pistol. Less accuracy.

And, critically, he had Claire. Gun to her head. Held mostly in front of himself.

Jade would need a rifle. And even then.

Jade started walking parallel to the bar. Angling toward the three at the bathroom door.

"I'd call this a standoff," she said.

The guy tracked her with his eyes. Dark green. Set deep in his head. As if he wore a permanent scowl.

"I have a gun." Jade kept walking. "You have a gun."

The guy kept watching. Kept the gun against Claire's head.

"We'd call that a standoff," Jade said.

She just needed for him to move it a fraction. Aim it at her.

Need Claire to drop out of the way.

"Except that I have an advantage." Jade kept

the gun aimed loosely at him.

She had no advantage at all. Not really.

"You know what that is?" she said.

The guy's eyes flicked toward the bar's windows.

"Not the cops," Jade said. "I realize that if you were worried about the cops you never would have come. You have an escape plan. The guy who sent you will make sure you get off, right?"

Uncertainty in his eyes.

He'd made a mistake. He'd grabbed Claire. The owner of *Bernie's Rest*. The local woman working hard to scratch out a living.

He should have grabbed Jade.

Big mistake.

Jade shifted her focus. Looked right into Claire's eyes.

Fear in there. A deep terror.

Jade bet there had been plenty of scuffles in *Bernie's Rest* over the years. Probably not often that there had been eight big guys carrying pistols shooting up the bathroom door.

Probably never had someone giving Claire a choke hold and pressing the cold muzzle of a gun to her head.

"Claire," Jade said. "It's going to be all right."

"Don't talk to her," the guy said.

From outside came the crunch of gravel under tires. The siren winding down. The flare of red and blue lights shone through the bar.

Jade didn't have long.

CHAPTER THIRTY SIX

The barroom was quiet. Jade could hear some breathing.

The cops' lights glinted from the bottles on the shelves up on the wall behind the bartop. Behind the big guy with his tree-trunk arm wrapped around Claire's neck.

The thing was to get the gun outside. Away from Claire.

The pair of them were behind the bar. Among the bottles and glasses. Beyond them the narrow door to the kitchen where Claire had reheated the burgers and thrown together the nachos.

The crunching of gravel had come to an end. The flashing of red and blue continued.

"What's your name?" Jade said.

The guy spat an epithet at her.

"You doing okay Claire?"

"Don't you talk to her!"

"You should leave," she said. "Door behind

you. Exit through the kitchen."

The guy glanced back.

Jade ducked. Not fast enough that he would get distracted, but fast enough that she was about out of his line of sight when he looked into the bar again.

He cursed again.

Then grunted.

The gun went off.

Jade stood bolt upright.

No sign of Claire.

The guy clutched at his jaw. He shook his head. He swung the gun down.

"Drop it!" Jade shouted.

He didn't.

He took a bead on her.

Jade fired. The bullet hit him square in the face.

He dropped. The gun fell with him.

Claire yelped.

"Petronas?" Jade yelled, already moving around the end of the bar. "Got them covered?"

"They're covered," he said. Calm. Assured.

From outside came the sound of a megaphone. Something about putting down weapons and coming out with hands locked on the top of your heads.

Jade kept moving. "Petronas? Can they see you?"

"I'm laying down now," he said. "Still got them covered."

"Good." Jade didn't want the cops looking through the window and firing on the one holding the gun.

Behind the bar the big guy lay twisted across Claire. Her right arm flailed as she tried to get out from under him.

The guy lay back. Mouth open wide. Gaze fixed on the ceiling. Right cheekbone crushed. Grisly meat showing.

Blood dripped from the hole in his face. And from the back of his head. No real flow.

The bullet had shut down his brain and heart in an instant. Nothing left pumping the blood out.

The whole point. With his gun aimed at her, Jade had to know that he wouldn't get off a reflex shot.

She didn't know how many people she'd killed over the years, but she knew it was only ever in circumstances like that.

Kill or be killed.

Jade grabbed his arm. Pulled him around. He was heavy. Probably somewhere north of two hundred pounds. Plenty of dense muscle.

But he rolled. Shifted almost off Claire.

Claire gasped. She sat up.

The guy's thighs still lay across her thighs.

"Nice reflexes," Jade said. She pulled at his legs.

Claire nodded. "Frankly, I just didn't want to be in the way when you shot him."

"Good thinking. I got to go check on Milton."

"You should go. Cops are here."

"Yeah. I'll let them in."

Another nod. Claire took a breath. She glanced at the body. "Nearly crushed me when he fell, though."

She met Jade's eyes and gave a half smile.

"I'll catch my breath," Claire said. "Go talk with them, then."

Jade hurried away.

The three guys cramped up at the bathroom door didn't even look at her.

Jade hurried to where she'd seen Milton fighting under the table.

They were still there. Both of them. Feet sticking out. Neither moving now.

Jade crouched right down. Peered under the table.

Milton lay underneath, head pressed against the wall. The guy lay across his chest, head against Milton's chin.

She saw blood on both faces.

"Milton?" she said. She hated to think.

He blinked. Stared at her. The whites of his eyes like tiny beacons.

"Kind of stuck here."

Jade saw that Milton had a choke hold on the guy. And the guy wasn't breathing. Any rise and fall came from Milton below.

"I think you can let now," Jade said.

"Uh-huh." Milton didn't let go.

"Come on. Let's get you out of there." Jade grabbed the second dead guy's boots and dragged him out. Milton shuffled. Jade couldn't tell whose blood was whose.

Milton pushed the body off. He moved into a sitting position.

"He had a knife," Milton said. He rubbed his left forearm. Caked in blood. A long gash ran toward the elbow.

Glad he was alive, Jade stood. "I'll go talk with the cops. You need a medic. Stay here."

"Yuh."

"Let me," Claire said.

Jade almost swung on her. She hadn't heard Claire come over. The woman had a small first aid kit.

"Thanks," Jade said. She headed for the door.

"Petronas?"

"Still got them covered."

"Good. Won't be but a minute now."

Jade interlinked her fingers. Put them on her head.

She stepped out into the cool night. A spotlight blazed in her eyes.

"It's me," she called. "Emily Jade."

"On your knees," someone shouted.

Jade complied.

"Derek Milton's inside," she said. "Hurt. You should get an ambulance."

"Stay where you are."

She let them cuff her.

Let them put her into the back seat of one of the cruisers. Time to let them take over now.

Leaning back into the cracked vinyl upholstery, Jade sighed. She could almost relax now.

Almost.

The thing was, who had set all this up? Gus? Claire?

Unlikely.

Looking over at the door, she saw the cops bringing someone else out in cuffs.

Gary Petronas.

Shouting at them. Trying to tell them he'd done nothing.

But of course they had to cuff him. He'd been holding a gun.

It would all work out.

But maybe they'd just made whoever was behind all this even madder.

Time to go find this Ivan Mortowitz.

CHAPTER THIRTY SEVEN

The engine of the Mercedes thrummed. Loud. Powerful.

For the first thirty minutes, Mortowitz drove fast. The Mercedes had excellent road handling. Excellent ride. One hundred felt like nothing more than fifty-five in any regular car. Better.

He kept the aircon on cool, aimed at his face.

He was sweating.

Not from any heat.

What had happened there? It should have been a simple thing to remove those last few links in the chain.

That woman investigator. No way of knowing what Sebastien had told her.

Had to be removed.

Officer Derek Milton. Helping her out.

Gary Petronas. The idiot investigator who thought he was doing Mortowitz a favor.

Mortowitz sighed. Sebastien should have just left it alone. Let it lie.

Mortowitz needed to do his own investigating, without anyone else getting in the way. Needed to find out just what Rich Cooper had done through all those transactions.

And how much of it could be traced back.

Tracing back that would probably lead directly to Mortowitz.

On a level it had been fine. On a nice, balance trajectory. Easy enough to monitor. Sebastien making very slow progress. Petronas ensuring that progress stayed throttled right back.

Manageable.

And now this woman. Somehow Sebastien had found some outside help.

Way outside.

An unknown quantity. Very little data on her.

Emily Jade. No known abode. Age indeterminate.

Very well hidden.

So far, proving very much a giant-sized spanner in the well-ordered works.

Shooting the Maeberry boys. Stopping Sandy.

And now creating mayhem with the team who'd come up from Jacksonville.

Hired muscle. Good reputation. Simple instructions. *No shooting. Hold her. Let me talk with her.*

And he'd walked right into a gunfight.

This was going to take something else. Something drastic.

He hated to think about it, but he was going to have to put in a call to Dallas.

The call of last resort.

Mortowitz kept driving. Distance was his friend right now.

And anything to put off making that call.

CHAPTER THIRTY EIGHT

Back at the Fernville City police building, in the spare office, Jade sipped on a bad coffee. A bustle of activity in the room. People from other agencies.

Lots of things to process here.

Two dead.

Three hospitalized.

Three in the cells out back. All of them vigorously exploiting their right to remain silent. All three of them had said not a word. All three of them had indicated with gestures that they wanted a pen and paper.

All three had written the same things. A name, *Nadine Cleghorn*. A third word, *Lawyer*. And a phone number.

The area code was for Jacksonville. Florida.

Well-drilled. Despite their rough and ready

appearance, all three of the guys had only one response.

Jade didn't doubt that the others–dead or otherwise–had been just as well-drilled.

Jade sat in the abandoned office, staring out into the pines. Wan light from the streetlamps crossed the building's roof and percolated through, giving the patch of forest an eerie feel.

Jade turned at a knock on the door. Milton. Blood wiped from his face. In a fresh shirt, but still civilian. No jacket. Shirt sleeve rolled up. Long, crisp white bandage covering his whole forearm.

"How's that doing?" she asked before he could say anything.

Milton glanced at his left arm as if he'd forgotten about the injury. He looked at her hand held up his right hand, thumb and index finger held close, showing a tiny gap. "Missed the artery by this much. Otherwise it's fine."

"And you should see the other guy."

"Not funny." Milton scowled and stepped into the room. "The other guy's dead. Because of me." Milton pulled around a chair from the wall. "I choked the life out of him."

Jade didn't speak. She felt for Milton. She wanted to say *It was either you or him* or *Self-defense*. But Milton knew that. He'd made the choice.

The guy had had a knife.

The difference between being alive or dead right now was that eighth of an inch.

What could have gone on in Milton's head? It all came down to *stop this guy slashing with the knife.*

"Have you got kids?" she said.

"Annette. She's doing something with chemistry and rocket fuel at JPL if you please. She doesn't talk to me much. It's getting better. I'm figuring she'll be just about over all that by the time she's twenty-five."

"Chemistry and rocket fuel?"

"Talking to her father. I said some stupid things when she was just doing what teenagers do. You know?"

"I know." Jade tried not to think about her own father. That it would have been nice to have had him say anything when she'd been a teenager. Nice to have had him around. At all.

"And now," Milton said, "you're going to tell me that it was kill or be killed. That it's better for my daughter to have her father still alive. Even if they're not on speaking terms."

"I'm not going to tell you something you already know. And the speaking terms is a one way thing, right? You'd be happy to speak with her."

"I'd get on a plane right now if she told me come over for a beer."

"JPL being on the west coast." The Jet Propulsion Laboratory. The place where they figured out how to fly into space on burning stacks of hydrocarbons.

"That's the one." Milton glanced at the floor and back at Jade. "I have the location locked in the GPS on my phone."

"Smart. I bet you have a rental car on standby at LAX and the route plotted."

Milton gave a sheepish grin. "Just about."

"You did the right thing. And mostly they survived. And they were the ones who brought guns. And started the shooting."

"We got duped," Milton said, face becoming serious.

"Petronas."

"That's what I thought. At first, maybe Claire. Maybe Gus."

"What happened to Gus?" Jade couldn't remember.

"I'll come to that." Milton blinked. "Do you need a refill?" He pointed at her coffee cup.

"It's late. Better not. I'm guessing it's a big day tomorrow."

"No bigger than today." Milton managed a smile. "This has been a day for the history books here."

"From the moment I rolled into town."

Milton stood. "I wouldn't phrase it like that. Mind if I grab a coffee?"

"Go ahead."

"Thanks. I'll run through everything in a moment."

The door clunked behind him.

Jade stared into the trees again. Intriguing how Milton was letting her get to know him just a fraction. He had a daughter ten years her junior. More or less.

It didn't make him any less appealing. Jade smiled, surprised at herself.

CHAPTER THIRTY NINE

The window glass in the small spare office had some smears. Probably not visible in daylight. Probably no one ever came in here after dark anyway.

Except for today.

"Gus," Milton said when he returned, "hid himself under the pool table."

The office smelled of Milton's rich, thick coffee. He hadn't used the standard percolator that sat out in the main office, but had brought in a plunger, and a small carton of long-life milk. Jade guessed he kept it all tucked away somewhere. A kind of emergency kit.

"There was no space under the pool table," Jade said. "Maybe two inches."

"There's a cavity in there. Gus ducked. Lifted off a side panel. Crept in."

"Big guy," Jade said, "but he's no idiot."

"I would have been in there with him, if I'd known."

"No you wouldn't."

Milton scowled. "Why do you say that? I'm as chicken as the next guy." He pressed the plunger on his coffee. The liquid swirled and the heavenly smell increased. Jade realized there was enough in the vessel for more than one cup.

"Because of your badge," she said. "You wouldn't be able to help yourself but get involved. As you proved."

"Right." Milton poured into his mug. He turned the plunger's spout toward Jade. "Sure you don't want a top up?"

Jade downed the rest of the plain coffee and let him fill her cup. "I'm wired enough to be up all night already."

"I bet." Milton set the plunger jug down, poured milk and offered her some, which she accepted.

Milton picked up her cup. He nodded at the window. "I like the setting of our little police station here. Almost right in the woods."

"It's pretty," Jade said.

"There's a fence out there. Captain Bainer got it put in after some trouble with the Maeberry family. Which I'm not supposed to tell you."

"About the fence?"

"About trouble with the family. The fence I can tell you all about. Something like fifteen feet back into the trees. Six feet high. Good Oregon pine, with steel railway iron uprights and razor wire coils along the top. Barbed wire strands on the inner side. Standard Hurricane wire mesh on the inner side too. And chain. Someone tries to chainsaw through the fence, they hit wire or the chain. Slows them down real fast."

"Has anyone tried?"

"Not that I know of."

"Seems like a pricey piece of construction for a little place. You could have just put cinderblocks this side of the trees. Cut down some of the trees even?"

"And ruin the ambience?" Milton took a big sip from his coffee.

"Of course not." Jade drank from her cup. Delicious. Best cup of coffee she'd had in North Carolina. On this trip, anyway.

"The captain had secured some Chamber of Commerce funding. Had to be spent. Longer story behind all that."

"I'm sure."

"Petronas claims to have no knowledge of the set up. Obvious to me that he's lying."

"He was the wrong person to speak with in the first place."

Milton raised his eyebrows. "Who then?"

"Maisie Souther."

"His clerk?"

"That's right. I'd lay even money that she's the real organization behind the outfit. Keeps it all running smoothly. Mr Petronas, bless him, intuits things. Looks for the advantage. Sees how things fit together. But he couldn't organize a business if someone gave him a hundred thousand dollars and the manual."

"I'd agree." Milton took another sip from his

cup. "So our next step is to go visit Maisie Souther?"

"That's right. What time is it now?"

"Close on midnight. You don't wear a watch? You don't even have a phone?"

"There are ways around those things. There's always someone with a phone. Or a payphone. Or some other way."

Milton smiled. "I'm starting to get the meaning of 'no fixed abode.'"

She gave him a smile. Everything she needed, really, resided in her head. Angus Webber's number. Internet access codes. Bank account numbers.

"Maisie Souther might still be up now?" Jade said.

"She might. I don't think she'd appreciate being woken. We can go check in the morning."

"Maybe. Where are you sleeping? I guess your place is still a crime scene. With everything going on around here, I can't imagine anyone's had any time to process it."

"That's right. Might be a day or two. The captain's given me a voucher for a motel. You can have it."

"What's the name of the motel?"

"Why?" Milton pulled out a yellow scrap of paper and looked at it.

"I saw a couple of places when I drove in," Jade said. "One I wouldn't stay at. I think the phrase is *be caught dead near*. The other place looked too pricey for a police department voucher."

"*Ocean Breeze*," he said. His eyes flicked to hers. "I'm guessing that's the place where you wouldn't be caught dead?"

Jade smiled. "Not that I have especially high standards, but I do like to sleep without getting bitten by bed critters, or woken by the neighbors' plumbing. Or other activities."

Milton just nodded.

"What about Sandy's place?" Jade said. "She won't be needing it."

Milton shuddered. "Let's call that off the table. And anyway, Captain wouldn't like it much. Not when I'll be tangled up in that investigation."

"Of course." Jade knew that would have been the case. She noticed that Milton barely reacted. "That leaves the other motel. I'm guessing there are just the two?"

"There are a couple if you make a right turn after the bridge to Tollis Island. Out on the shore."

"Any better than *Ocean Breeze*?"

"I don't think so."

"Let's try the other place I saw." Jade took another sip from her coffee. It really was very good. Too bad it was so late at night. "You want to tag along? I can spring for a room."

Milton held up the voucher. "I guess I'd better use this."

"It's not charity. We're partnering up here."

"I... get that." Milton scratched his mustache. Dropped his hand. "But..." He sighed. "All right then."

"But what?"

"Captain will ask questions. You and I at the same motel. Doesn't matter."

"Okay. I get it. Do you want a ride out there? They're less than a half a mile apart."

"Sure. Captain can't say anything about that."

CHAPTER FORTY

Out front of the police building Jade looked up at the stars. They shone bright. The dim lights of Fernville City didn't block out much. The air was cool.

She leaned back against the rental truck. Solid and reassuring.

Milton followed her out.

"All right," he said, and climbed in on the passenger side.

Jade went around and started the engine.

"One stop first," Milton said as they pulled away from the police building. The truck's engine thrummed.

"Okay." Jade pulled into the empty roadway and drove away from the town square.

"You're not disagreeing? You're not saying you need to sleep?"

"I do need to sleep," Jade said. "But we didn't go and see Maisie Souther."

"So you knew what I meant already?"

"That's what I'm doing here."

"Okay." Milton gave her directions.

Driving to Maisie Souther's place involved traveling less than two miles. Some through countryside, some through the sparse neighborhoods. Milton knew the way.

Maisie Souther lived in a double-wide on what had to be an acre of land. In the dark, Jade could see mostly tree silhouettes, but also the lights of the nearest neighbors.

Jade's headlights lit up a well-kept bronze-colored Ford Taurus standing in a carport built onto the side of the building. On a concrete pad. A row of succulents in hand-painted pots overflowed, growing lush and fast.

Maisie Souther wasn't home.

"Probably a good sign," Milton said, standing on the cinderblock doorstep. He knocked again anyway.

"Probably," Jade said. She suppressed a yawn.

"We can track her down in the morning." Milton stepped down. "You need rest. I need rest."

"We're not any good to anyone dead tired."

"That's what I was thinking."

The sound of rigging snapping against a mast came from nearby. Jade realized that the property backed onto the waterway. Probably a yacht moored at a buoy or a jetty, rocking in the waves. She could smell the tang salt in the air.

"Let's go to the motel," Milton said. "Start fresh first thing."

As they got back into the truck, Jade saw a

flashlight glint in the rearview mirror. Someone walking along the driveway.

"Someone's coming," she said.

She sensed Milton tense. He looked around through the truck's rear window.

"Pretty casual," he said.

"That's how it seemed." Jade opened the door and called out, "Hello."

"Hello there!" the bearer of the flashlight said. Male. Probably in his sixties or seventies from the tenor of the voice. Local. "You're looking for Maisie."

"That's right," Jade said.

"Not around. Are you cops? I don't know you."

Jade still hadn't seen his face. Lost in the glare from the flashlight.

"I'm from out of town. Helping out with some of the things going on around here. He's a cop, though."

Milton stepped out of the truck. "Hi."

"Officer Milton," the man said. "I think I've spoken with you before. When that kid fell off the boat out back of my property."

"Couple years back," Milton said. "You're Joseph Douglas."

"Joe." The man stepped forward, holding out his hand. "Been quite a day, from what I hear."

"Yes it has." Jade stayed standing by the truck as Milton and Joe Douglas shook hands. "You're a neighbor of Maisie's?"

The flashlight beam darted to the right. "That place right there. Used to be able to walk right across, but that last storm turned a whole big patch there into bottomless bog so I gotta walk around the driveways." The beam darted back along the gravel track, then onto the truck's tray again.

"Do you know where Maisie's gotten to?"

"She got a call," Joe said. "Earlier on. She came by, asked if I could feed her cat for a couple of days. She seemed in a hurry."

"Oh. She didn't say where she was headed?"

"Nope. I think that might have been part of the point."

"We were hoping to get hold of her. Ask her some questions."

"Kind of late in the day for that. Pretty sure everyone should be tucked up asleep by now. Me included."

"Yes. Us too. But we do want to make sure she's safe."

"She's in danger?"

"We don't know. But she might have some of the answers we're looking for."

"Okay. She didn't mention anything to me. If she shows up, I'll let her know you're looking for her, Officer Derek Milton and…"

"Jade. Emily Jade."

"All right. I suppose she can just call the police station and leave a message then?"

"That would work. But maybe my cell." Milton fished in his pocket and took out a card. He passed it to Joe Douglas.

"Well then. I suppose that concludes our business. I hope you all have a better day tomorrow."

"Likewise." Joe Douglas shone his flashlight along the driveway and headed away.

"Friendly," Jade said to Milton.

"We're that kind of community."

"Could have fooled me so far."

"Ah, you're basing your opinion on too small a sample."

Jade climbed back into the truck. "I'm counting a sample of something like twelve people with guns so far. Seems like plenty to me."

"Come on, enough of that. Let's go find somewhere to sleep."

CHAPTER FORTY ONE

The *Ocean Breeze* was a two-story cinder-block edifice that would never win any architectural prizes. Standard motel layout, with a row of alternating doors and windows along the first floor and the balcony. Stairways at either end accessed the balcony. Jade saw a section where the railing had broken away and been repaired with an old wooden pallet.

"Charming," Milton said.

They headed to the office, which smelled of burgers and had a rack of faded brochures for companies that had probably gone out of business a decade back.

It turned out that the *Ocean Breeze* motel had no rooms left anyway. "*Banks View* is closed up," the tired clerk told them. At the end of the cramped lobby a dark soda machine held up a handwritten sign that read *Out of Order*.

"*Banks View*?" Jade said.

"One of the motels out on Tollis Island. Refurbishing. They have to every few years. We get the overflow."

"Guess you're with me," Jade said to Milton as they headed out to her Ford.

"Other place might be full up too."

But it wasn't. The *Sixteen Palms* had a clean heated pool, a hot tub, vending machines that worked and twelve other vehicles parked in near side of the lot. Mostly pickups like Jade's. The clerk wore a business shirt and tie. The polished counter looked like old oak.

Jade used her credit card to pay for two rooms. Three times, at least, the value of Milton's voucher.

"You do carry something on you," he said.

"Yes I do."

"I'll pay you back."

"Okay." She wouldn't let him anyway.

The *Sixteen Palms* was a two story affair that reminded Jade of a Best Western. Beige walls, thick carpet, a breakfast room with facilities for more than just donuts and coffee. Perhaps a failed franchise, rebranded by a local entrepreneur.

Their rooms were upstairs side by side, but without connecting doors.

"I only have the clothes I'm wearing," Milton said, standing in the open doorway to his room.

"Likewise. Shower, sleep. Hang your clothes on the back of the chair so they air out. You can grab a fresh outfit in the morning. Surely they'll let you home to get a change of clothes?"

"Maybe." Milton stared at her for a moment.

Gazes locked.

"You want to spend some time discussing the next move?"

He gave a wry smile and a slight nod. "I think that would be both a good idea and problematic."

"Problematic?" Jade liked his eyes. The clarity and uncertainty in them at once. Too old for her, but then it didn't have to be anything serious.

"We're tired," Milton said. "We should talk when we're fresh."

"I won't sleep much," Jade said. "I'm aware of the truck in the motel lot."

Milton frowned. "The truck?"

"We parked it at the bar. Where the ruckus went down. Now the same truck is parked here." Jade pointed toward the front of the motel.

"Ruckus." Milton took a breath and closed his eyes. "Okay."

"So it's obvious where I am. If someone was looking."

"You think they're looking? You think there are still more out there?"

"Yes."

"You should park it around back."

"Wouldn't help. Might have been seen on the road. That clerk at *Ocean Breeze* saw us. Knows there's only one other option. Really."

Milton huffed. "The way your head works." He glanced into his room. "Are you going to play sentry?"

"For awhile. First I've got to go move the truck."

"Move it?"

"To a parking space right outside the room. So

I can watch if anyone comes."

"You think they'll do something to the truck?"

"I think they'll try to confirm that they have the right truck."

Milton nodded. "Lots of pickups around town."

"And in the motel's parking lot."

Another nod. "You're right. I didn't notice that. Tired."

"You should get some sleep."

"You too. Let me take first watch."

"Really? You're dead on your feet. How about you come and wake me in a couple of hours."

Another nod. He watched her for a moment, then said, "See you then."

Milton slipped into his room and closed the door with a thud. Jade turned and went to move the truck. She found one space, a couple of parks along from right below her room. The view would work.

As she relocked the vehicle, a black sedan pulled around from the back of the motel. The car stopped in behind her truck. Blocking its exit, and that of the cars either side.

Two men in business suits stepped out. One tall, one average height. Both younger than Jade.

The near one stayed where he was. The other one came around the car to join him. The suits bulged at the chest. Left side, as if they carried guns.

"Are you Emily Jade?" the shorter one said.

"Yes I am."

"Then you should come with us."

CHAPTER FORTY TWO

A cool wind blew a burger wrapper across the parking lot tarmac. Jade glanced up at the motel building behind. Each room either had no lights on, or curtains closed.

People asleep. No one watching what was happening outside.

No one to notice the new arrivals.

The black sedan was a Chevy Impala. The engine sounded smooth, but with an underlying power. The interior smelled of leather polish.

The taller guy drove. He exited the motel's parking lot already doing thirty-five.

"You're not Mortowitz's people," Jade said.

Neither of them spoke. The car headed inland.

"Not going to tell me what this is about? My mother warned me about getting into cars with strange men."

"We're not strange," the shorter one said.

"I should have asked to see your ID."

"Wouldn't have done any good."

"ID can be faked," the driver said. "You couldn't tell the difference."

"Anyway, we know you well enough to know that you improvise."

"I was going to go to sleep. The day I've had."

"We know about your day."

"And," the driver said, "you weren't planning on sleeping."

"I wasn't?"

"You were going to watch for Mortowitz's people."

"Why do you say that? You didn't see the bed. And as tired as I am I could have slept on the floor."

Jade rubbed at a pinch in her shoulder. Milton would be expecting her to wake him sometime.

What would happen if Mortowitz's people did arrive?

"Why did you shift the truck?" the short guy said. He had a clean-shaven face, with clear skin. As if he'd only been shaving for less than a year.

Jade smiled. "Got me. Who are you? State police? FBI."

"That doesn't matter."

"Sure it does."

"We're investigators."

"Which says nothing. Private? Nice car for that line of work."

Neither of them spoke.

"Where are you taking me?"

Nothing.

Jade sat back and looked through the windows. Nighttime North Carolina flashed by.

Farms. Stands of trees. A few buildings. She glimpsed a cat stalking along a wooden fence.

Fifteen minutes from the motel, the car pulled onto a gravel driveway. Ditches on either side. No way to turn around. No way to get by a vehicle coming the other way. Ahead a light shone.

As they approached the light grew into aporch light on a two story farm house. White with a long veranda. Dark roof with three sets of dormer windows. Lights on inside two of them.

Another vehicle parked out front. In the headlight beams, Jade saw that the second vehicle was an identical Impala. Dark blue, not black.

The Impala could seat five. There could be ten of them here. Or just these two, one car each and they'd picked her up together for efficiency.

Or a whole lot more. The vehicles might had done shuttle runs.

"What is this place?" she said as the car slowed, pulling into park next to its twin.

"It's a local monitoring set-up."

"Monitoring what?"

"Locals."

"Is that supposed to be a joke?"

No response.

The car came to a stop. The tall guy pressed the button to shut the car off. The engine fell silent.

No one moved.

From out in the dark a bird called. It might have been an owl. Hunting rodents.

"Is this about Ivan Mortowitz?" Jade said.

"Come inside."

Jade knew both of them were armed.

She looked at the house. It could have been any farmhouse around the area. Big enough for a family of eight. Constructed well enough to last a hundred and twenty years. If the owners took care of it.

"What's inside," she said.

"Answers."

The two guys opened their doors at the same time. They stepped out.

Jade stayed where she was.

The two guys stayed where they were. After a moment, the shorter one said something. She didn't catch the words.

The taller guy replied, likewise unintelligible.

The shorter guy barked a reply and leaned in through the front passenger door. "What?" he said to Jade, staring right at her.

"I need more information here. You have to understand, I'm way out on a limb."

"You're not on a limb. You could disarm us and disable us in a heartbeat."

"Possibly."

"We've seen you in action. We're asking for your help."

"Funny way of asking."

"Come inside, please. We're on a timeline here."

"Is anyone watching the motel?"

"The motel?"

"Officer Derek Milton is asleep there. Alone."

"We have eyes on the motel."

"Watching for Mortowitz's people?"

"That's just about all we do now."

That surprised Jade. "You're bringing me onboard? Into something much bigger. Bigger than Rich Cooper's disappearance?"

"You already know that it's bigger than that."

"I was starting to suspect. But he's a key element."

"Come inside."

"Who are you?"

The shorter guy ducked out again and conferred again with the taller one. The taller one gave a clear and terse, "No!"

The shorter guy looked back in. "It's complicated," he said.

"I bet. I'm not getting out until I know." Stupid move. If she was planning on not getting out of the car, she should have not gotten into it in the first place.

Should have gone back up to get Milton too.

Tired. More than tired. Exhausted.

Beyond measure.

Shouldn't have even considered keeping watch. Should have parked the truck off some lane a mile from the motel and walked back.

Gotten some sleep.

Now here she was. Out miles from anywhere. Two armed men either side of her. Who knew how many back in that house.

Tactical error. The kind of error you only made once. Because you didn't survive that first time to make it a second time.

"Wait here," the guy said.

He pulled back out of the car. Walked toward the house.

Jade sat waiting.

The tall guy stood waiting.

The bird called again.

Cool air rolled into the car through the open door.

Jade waited.

The guy waited.

Jade saw him move. Just a slight turn of the head.

Jade looked around at the house.

Someone stepped from the front door. Out onto the veranda. Into the light.

A woman. She pointed at Jade, lifted her hand. Made a single beckoning waved.

Turned and disappeared back inside.

CHAPTER FORTY THREE

In the same way that the car's interior had smelled of leather polish, the house's interior smelled of furniture polish. Pledge. Pine. Maybe a hint of cilantro too, and chili, as if someone had spent the last hour cooking.

The short guy stood just inside the entry. A wide stairway led to the second floor. Framed pictures hung on the wall all the way up.

"This way," the guy said. He pointed to Jade's left, indicating a living room. Polished wooden floors. Wide Persian rug in the center. High-backed antique chairs with wooden frames and patterned upholstery. Coffee table. Tall china cabinet against the wall.

As she stepped through, Jade glimpsed a third man. Down the corridor at the kitchen entry. Medium build. Wearing a white apron.

"Go on," the short man said behind her.

The woman sat in one of the chairs. Facing the front of the house. Waiting. She wore a skirt business suit that wouldn't have been out of place in the 1960s. Big collar, black skirt reaching to just above the knees.

Jade walked through. "I didn't dress up," she said, looking around. On one wall hung a big oil painting of sunrise across the ocean, dunes in the foreground, a yacht in in the water.

"I wouldn't have expected that," the woman said. She sounded English.

"Who are you?" Jade said.

The woman simply smiled.

"Why am I here?" Jade said.

"Ivan Mortowitz."

"What's your interest?"

"Competition."

"Competition."

The woman smiled. She had very straight teeth. Somewhere north of sixty, but in good shape. No surgery, but she looked after herself. Trim, smooth skin, bright eyes. Maybe she had had a little work done around the eyes.

"Ivan Mortowitz is an oaf," the woman said. "And he interferes with my business interests. It's irritating to say the least."

"People are dying."

"There you are."

"I'd call that more than irritating. Not for you. For them. *To say the least*. I don't know you or your *interests*, but it seems to me that someone needs to back down."

Another smile. A nod. "Or perhaps someone

needs to be out of the picture."

"You're talking about me?"

"I'm talking about Mortowitz."

"Mortowitz." Things started to make sense to Jade. This woman was in competition with Mortowitz.

Interesting.

"He's out of control. We have some good systems in place around here. In general we stay out of each other's way. This last year has been somewhat problematic. I'm not convinced that Mr Mortowitz is entirely stable. Would you like something to drink? Juice? Water? Coffee or tea at this time of night would disagree with my system, and I'm sure yours too. As would any alcohol."

"Sure," Jade said. "Water, please."

The woman glanced to her left and made a slight wave. A moment later the shorter guy came in with a tray. On the tray stood two bottles of Dasani water, and two tumblers.

He set the tray on the coffee table and departed. Jade uncapped one of the bottles and poured. Into both tumblers. She picked one up and drank, surprised by how thirsty she was.

"Did you leave someone to watch over the motel?" Jade said. "To see if those guys track the truck?"

A blink. Hesitation.

Jade stood. "I think you should take me back. I don't think I can help you."

"But I can help you."

"Really? It doesn't seem like it."

"Ed Herlihy," the woman said. "Maisie

Souther. Even Jodie Clemons. You talk to them yet?"

"Herlihy's dead. That's what I heard."

"That's right."

"Maisie Souther's missing. We went to her place." Jade told the woman about Joe Douglas arriving up the driveway with his flashlight.

"Okay. I'm sure you can find her."

"Likewise."

"So maybe you should go talk to Jodie Clemons soon too. She knew Rich Cooper. She's been alright up until now." The woman reached and picked up the second tumbler. She sipped. "Things are heating up."

"Meaning you might come under the microscope?"

"Meaning that Officer Derek Milton is not the only one you need to keep safe."

Jade nodded. "I understand."

"Good. What's your number? I'd like to pass on some information once I get it. Help you find these two."

"I don't have a phone."

The woman raised her eyebrows. "That's very... unusual." She glanced at the door again and made the little wave.

A moment later, the short guy came back, carrying a slim phone. He placed it on the coffee table in front of Jade. The phone's screen glowed.

"It's a burner," the woman said. "I believe that's what they call them."

Jade gave a small shake of her head. "How about this?" She gave the woman one of Angus

Webber's numbers. "Call. Leave a message. I can retrieve it."

"This would be more convenient."

"I appreciate the thought," Jade said. "But I don't want to be in your debt. Don't want to get in over my head."

"Too late for that, my dear, but as you wish." The woman stood. She stepped around the chair. "I'll leave you a message. I suppose that can work." Without another glance, the woman left the room, heading into the back of the house.

Jade looked at the shorter guy still standing in the doorway.

"We can go now," he said.

"Yes," Jade said. That it was time to go was obvious anyway.

CHAPTER FORTY FOUR

The two guys with the Impala delivered Jade back to the motel. She saw that the truck still sat out in the lot. She made her way straight to Milton's room.

He answered even while she was still hammering on his door. He had a towel clasped at his waist.

"Little late," he said. He seemed bleary and tired. "Time for my shift?"

Jade filled him in on the encounter with the woman.

"You know who she is?" Milton said.

"I figured you would."

A shake of his head. "This is new to me. I vaguely knew about Mortowitz. He stayed under the radar, I guess. This woman's not even airborne."

"A radar metaphor," Jade said. "Okay. She wants to help. But for her own gain. I know that."

"You were worried she might track you with the phone? GPS and so on?"

"That was one aspect. I didn't want to be obligated to her."

"I like your attitude."

"Sleep now," Jade said. "I'll see you in the morning."

"What about sentry duty?"

"Don't need it."

"Why do you say that?"

"Hunch. Maisie's disappeared. This woman found us. I think Mortowitz is truly regathering."

"Two big setbacks today. For Mortowitz."

"Three, if you count Sandy."

"Which we should."

"So he's really got to regather. No troops left."

"We hope."

Milton nodded. "Chain your door. Put a chair behind it. Call me room to room if you have any troubles."

"And you do likewise."

"You can count on it."

Again their eyes lingered. Jade smiled.

"I'll see you in the morning." Milton turned and stepped back into his room. Without looking again, he closed his door.

Jade went into her own room. She chained the door. She went to the curtains and looked out at the truck. Still where she'd left it.

And out on the road, across the other side, where she could only just see it, sat the blue-black Impala. Interior dark. The car only visible as a silhouette.

Jade pulled the curtains closed. She stripped

and showered. She dried off and slumped onto the bed.

She let sleep overtake her.

Morning light woke her. When she looked out through the curtains, the Impala was gone.

So was the truck.

And when she knocked on Milton's door he didn't answer.

CHAPTER FORTY FIVE

The motel's hallway smelled of carpet shampoo. The carpet looked generic. The same basic pattern could go in any medium-range hotel.

Jade pounded on Milton's door a moment longer. No answer. Returning to her own room, she used the phone to call direct to his room.

No answer.

Nor any answer when she knocked on the door between their rooms.

Jade returned to the hallway. Milton still didn't answer when she pounded on his main room door there.

A twenty-something jock came out of his own room a couple of doors down. Shirtless, with thick shoulders and washboard abs, the jock watched her as he took a few steps along the hallway.

He stopped at the vending machine and

dropped in a few coins. The machine clunked and whirred and delivered him an overpriced soda. The jock took the can, popped the top. The can hissed. He sipped, staring at her.

"You know," he said, "if whoever you're looking for was in there, they would have answered already." He glanced back along the hallway. "'cause you woke me up all the way down there and let me tell you, I can sleep."

Jade said nothing. She just stared at him until he shrugged, turned and returned to his room. He flipped her the bird as he disappeared through the door.

Jade knew he was right.

Downstairs, she asked at the front desk.

No, they hadn't seen him leave. No, he hadn't checked out. No they couldn't let her into the room. No they couldn't call the police, but she was welcome to do so.

"Really?" she said.

"Let me call the manager."

"Sure." Jade left. She walked around the motel twice.

Back in her room she called Angus Webber.

Angus picked up on the third ring. "Some mess you've got going on down there."

"Yeah, thanks. I try."

"What can I do?"

Jade told him about Milton's disappearance.

"You weren't around?" Angus sounded more alert.

"I had to make a visit." She launched into another quick explanation about the blue Impala and the woman. And about giving the number for the message service.

"Good idea. People can track you with those phones these days."

"I figured. Who is she? Would she take Milton too?"

"Why didn't you call me last night?"

Jade didn't answer.

After a moment, Webber said, "I understand. But there's no sense in you getting yourself mired in something with no way out."

"I don't need rescuing."

"I know that. I couldn't pull off a rescue anyway."

Jade sighed. "And I know that. That's not exactly why I didn't call. I figure you need sleep. You help me plenty anyway. Finding me jobs. Finding details about my father."

"I tell you this too often, Emily. You can call me anytime."

"I know."

"So do."

"Yes. Will."

"Which you say every time too."

"Yeah." Jade smiled to herself. Webber was about the only person who called her Emily.

"Give me fifteen minutes," he said. "I'll get you some data."

"One other thing that's occurred to me too. A photo from Sebastien's wall. A guy in a picture with Rich Cooper. It seemed important."

"A guy? Anything more."

"A name. Let me think." It took her a moment. "Coleman D. Gardner. From Charleston. West Virginia."

"I know where Charleston is."

Jade smiled. "Can you do that too?"

"Fifteen minutes, like I said."

"I'll call you then."

"Stay where you are. I'll call you."

"At the motel?"

"You still tired."

"Sure. I can sleep tomorrow."

"Shower. Go grab some breakfast while it's still on downstairs. Be back by the phone in fifteen minutes."

Jade paused a beat. Sometimes she just needed to wait. "Okay," she said. "Talk to you in fifteen."

CHAPTER FORTY SIX

The motel's breakfast buffet was well laid out. Cereals and bagels, coffee and juice, fruit and a big heater tray with lamps, holding eggs, bacon, sausage, tomato and mushrooms.

Jade loaded up a plate with proteins and sugars and carried it past the frowning desk clerk on back up to the room.

She ate through the sausages, eggs, and bagel, sitting by the phone. For motel food it was surprisingly good. Jade wished that she could have spent more time. A leisurely hour down in the breakfast room, chatting with the other guests. Sampling yoghurt and fruit.

The phone rang.

Jade set down her fork and answered.

"You should come down here sometime," she said. "This breakfast is great."

"Motel breakfast," Webber said. "No thanks."

"I was kind of kidding. We have different

tastes."

"Coleman D. Gardner, of Charleston, West Virginia. Dead end."

"Dead?"

"No. On deployment. Now, and back when Rich Cooper vanished. I'm not supposed to know, but he's in Israel right now. No way to get a hold of him."

"Israel?"

"It's nothing. I promise you."

"All right. The woman?"

"I've got nothing there either," Webber said. "Don't know who she is. I'm real sorry."

"That's kind of what I was wondering. She's anonymized herself."

"Yes. If I had another day, I'm sure we could come up with something."

"So keep hunting at your end. I'll keep hunting at mine."

"I might have a lead on your missing cop. And your missing rental truck."

"Well, those sure would be useful."

"Just call the station. I think you'll find him there."

Jade raised her eyebrows in surprise. "Simple as that?"

"Not quite. His captain hauled him in. From what I can see. Something's going down."

"Something?"

"You might want to get over there."

"All right." Jade stood. She took another forkful of breakfast.

"Call me soon, okay?" Webber said. "Give me updates."

"Will do."

Jade hung up. She should have thought of that. And of course she didn't need to get down to the station immediately. She could just call.

The front desk connected her. They would bill her room, but it was quicker than going through directory service.

She might be the only one in the world left who actually ever used directory service.

The police department's desk clerk answered. Polite and clear. Jade asked for Officer Derek Milton.

"He's in a meeting right now. So... wait a moment, he's looking over at me. Waving. Could you call back?"

"I can wait," Jade said. She figured out how to make the room phone switch to speaker. She pressed the button and set the receiver down on the night table.

"No, wait," the desk clerk said, voice both crisp and distant through the phone's external speaker.

"I'm not going anywhere," Jade said.

"He wants to speak with you. Here you are."

"Jade?" Milton said. "You're awake?"

"Awake and wondering what's going on."

"Captain Bainer hauled me in. Turns out we're pretty busy."

"Figured that might happen."

"There's new information? "

"Yes there is."

"Didn't the front desk tell you? At the motel?"

"No. You left a message?" Jade recalled the desk clerk watching her leave the buffet with a plate crammed with food.

"Doesn't matter now. I didn't want to wake you. Remember Ealing Cooper? Rich's nephew."

"One of the guys who torched Sebastien's place?"

"The very one. He's decided to talk."

"Well that's something." Jade looked at her plate of food, wishing that she had just gotten a yoghurt.

"Come down here when you're ready," Milton said. "I can do that thing of, you know, *read you in*, but I can give you some details."

"All right. Did you take the truck?" On the night table next to the phone lay the truck keys. How would he have taken it?

"The truck?"

"It's not where I parked it," Jade said.

"Interesting." Milton said something away from the phone. Jade couldn't make out the words. "All right," he said clearly. "Everything's stretched thin as cling wrap here, but we'll get someone to pick you up. I guess you'll have to report the truck stolen too."

"No one's ever going to rent to me again."

Milton was speaking away from the phone again. Then to her, "No it's fine. Not your fault. Listen, there's already a car out your way. Cadence will pick you in a couple of minutes. I'll see you in fifteen."

"Cadence?" Jade said, but Milton had already hung up.

CHAPTER FORTY SEVEN

Jade waited out on the sidewalk in front of the motel. Thick clouds built overhead, as if the weather was planning a rainstorm for later.

Cars and trucks slipped by fast, leaving a constant buzz of traffic noise. Across the road in a vacant lot a crow pecked at something on the ground.

A police car pulled up at the curb on Jade's side.

Cadence turned out to be a cop in her mid-forties. Trimmed blonde hair, and a trim figure. Jade might have seen her in passing yesterday. Cadence invited Jade to ride up front.

"Just don't touch anything."

"Wouldn't dream of it," Jade said.

Cadence drove quick, darting the police cruiser out into the thin traffic and barreling along just above the posted limit. The racked shotgun in the center console rattled.

"Yesterday was quite a day," Cadence said. She smelled of talcum powder. She glanced at Jade. "Hoping today's nothing like that."

"Likewise," Jade said.

The car rode over a pothole. The screens facing Cadence's seat shook in their brackets.

"You're that investigator from out of state, aren't you?"

"I am."

"Bring it all with you?"

"I truly didn't mean to."

"Sorry, I didn't mean to snap at you."

"No. It's all right."

"I'm supposed to be having the week off. Captain called me back in first thing. Just for a couple of hours, he said. Just to run a couple of regular patrols. I can see that turning into all day."

Jade didn't say anything. The road was a four-lane, with a striped buffer through the center. A few tarmac patches here and there. Businesses along the shoulder. Car valet, kitchenware supplier, lumber yard. A few secondhand car dealers. More than a few empty, weedy lots.

A steady stream of cars traveled both directions. Cadence drove in the fast lane. Aware of the effect of the presence of the police cruiser on the driving habits of others.

Jade sensed Cadence glance over. Jade turned to meet her eyes. Cadence smiled.

"My daughter," Cadence said. "Della. Just had her first child. I've been helping out. Born two days ago. She needs all the help she can get. Ratfink father lit out for Texas two weeks back. Says he'll send money. Going to work on the oil rigs, he thinks."

"You don't think so?"

"I think he suddenly realized that changing diapers at midnight wasn't quite his thing. Figures that Grandma will pitch in. Tell you what, next time Grandma sees the little fink she'll teach him how to change diapers all right."

Jade smiled.

"So, that was my week. Changing diapers. Suddenly I'm Della's mom again, after being, you know, a drag. More than fine with me. Too bad I'm back at work."

"I'll have a word to the captain. If that would help?"

Another broad smile. "You know, maybe it actually would."

Ahead Jade saw a truck approaching on the other side. A Ford F-150. Same color as her rental.

As the truck drew closer Jade focused on the license tag.

Her truck.

She pointed. "That's my truck."

CHAPTER FORTY EIGHT

Ivan Mortowitz almost idled his Mercedes along the driveway leading toward Madeleine Howarphe's ostentatious farmhouse. Morning light shone through the trees. In one of the nearby fields a tall dark brown stallion stood. The animal flexed its withers and shook its mane.

The closest thing Howarphe would ever come to actual farming. Raising a few horses.

Of course the farm, such as it was, formed nothing more than a front. *Another* front.

Mortowitz pulled up in front of the house. Typical white clapboard, with verandas and attic windows. The kind of place photographers used to portray the idea of an idyllic country life.

Marred, of course, by the two black-blue sedans parked out front. They betrayed the façade. Nothing that happened behind those walls had anything to do with the idyllic.

Mortowitz smiled to himself as he stopped the car. They were birds of a feather, him and Howarphe. Both looking out for their own best interests.

And here he was, almost trying to extending an olive branch. A temporary thing.

Just until all this had blown over.

Taking a breath, Mortowitz stepped out onto the gravel. His shoes crunched in the gravel. The scents of the countryside wafted at him. Pollen. Animals. Fresh paint. Perhaps she repainted the house every year. It glowed as white as an actor's teeth.

He'd only taken one step from the car when someone called at him to stop.

From the left of the house.

Mortowitz looked across. A short man in a dark suit stood there. Mortowitz recognized him. Didn't know the name, but he was one of Horwarphe's personal crew.

"I need to talk to her," Mortowitz said.

"I doubt that it's mutual," the man said. He had his hands simply clasped at his crotch. A pistol held there. In his right hand. Muzzle pointed to the left.

It would take about a quarter second to rise to chest level and fire.

"Maybe I could ask her myself?" Mortowitz said.

"How about this?" The man started walking toward Mortowitz. "How about you leave me your card and I'll pass it on to her? Then, she can call you at her convenience."

"This will all come back on her, you know?"

"I think that's for her to de—"

"It's okay, Sam," Madeleine Howarphe said from the veranda, stepping through the house's front door. "I don't see the harm in a conversation."

She came down the steps.

"Madeleine," Mortowitz said.

"Ivan. What a supreme shambles you've created. All over one simple botched disposal."

Mortowitz said nothing. He knew she was right.

"What can I do for you?" Howarphe said.

"I need to get Ealing Cooper out of police hands."

"Cooper being the only one besides you who knows where the body is buried, correct?"

Mortowitz took a breath.

"What's in it for me?" Howarphe said.

"Fifty percent of my business."

"Seems like a lot, but it's not enough."

"Please."

Howarphe shrugged. "It's already in hand. We're getting Cooper out. Why don't you come inside and we'll negotiate those terms more precisely?"

"I'm happy to negotiate out here."

Mortowitz saw the short guy's hands unclasp. The gun hand rose. The muzzle pointed right at Mortowitz's feet.

"Sorry," Howarphe said with an evil smile. "I didn't catch that."

Mortowitz sighed again. "All right. Inside."

He followed Howarphe into the house.

CHAPTER FORTY NINE

From the passenger seat of Cadence's police car, Jade stared at her rental truck. On the opposite side. Heading inland.

Beyond the truck a boatyard stood next to a hardware supply store.

It all seemed too weird. Just a pickup truck driving along the highway.

Except that it was hers.

"Your truck?" Cadence said, watching traffic.

"Right there." Jade pointed.

Craning forward, she leaned against the police car's hard dash. She watched the truck's driver.

Scruffy beard. Dark glasses. Aviators. A beat-up black cap.

Gone. Speeding off in the other direction.

Twisting, Jade watched the truck.

"My rental." Jade clung to the seat's cool upholstery, staring through the grate and the rear window. The truck moved easily along through the light traffic.

"Can we follow it?" she said.

"I gotta bring you back," Cadence said.

But Jade felt the car slow. She heard the *tick, tick, tick* of the turning indicator.

Cadence pulled the wheel. Swung across to the other side. She left her sirens and lights off. But she accelerated hard. Put herself in the outside lane. Came up within a few car lengths of the truck.

"Take the mic," Cadence said. "Call it in."

"Am I allowed to do that?"

"No. But go ahead. You sure it's your truck?"

"Certain."

They were approaching a crossroads. A high, flashing orange light suspended on cables over the middle. A couple of cars waiting on the right. Main road traffic continuing through. A CVS on the corner with a few cars in the lot.

The truck slowed.

Jade took the radio's microphone. The cord dangled.

"Why's he slowing down?" Cadence said.

"Fernville City police department?" Jade said. "This is Emily Jade. Can I speak with Officer Milton?"

"Pass it to me," Cadence said.

"Receiving you," the radio's speaker said. "Is that you Cadence?"

Jade handed Cadence the mic. "Yes," Cadence said into it. "I'm now following Emily Jade's stolen rental. Not quite a 10-80 yet. Making a right from highway seventy onto Bullwark road.

Heading north."

"Copy that. You need assistance?"

"Not yet. We'll keep you posted." Cadence handed the mic back.

The truck accelerated, turned hard. Cut off another car.

Cadence cursed. She accelerated after the truck. The police car bumped as it changed to the other roadway. A woman standing at a car in the CVS parking lot stared at them.

"I've got a phone," Cadence said. She stayed close behind the truck. It kept picking up speed.

Cadence kept one hand on the wheel. With her other hand she reached into a pouch at her waist. She pulled out a slim white phone. She passed it to Jade.

"The lock code is one-two-three-four," Cadence said.

"Seriously?" But Jade tapped in the code. The phone's screen sprang to life with an array of icons. Jade tapped to make a call.

Cadence's contacts came up. Jade pressed the *D* and several names appeared. Including Derek Milton's.

The truck continued accelerating away. They passed through another intersection. The truck didn't slow. Cadence did.

Jade made the connection. Pressed the phone to her ear. The phone rang.

One ring. Two.

"This guy's speed is creeping up here," Cadence said.

Three rings.

"I'm think I'm going to have to pull him over."

Four rings.

Jade watched the truck make a turn. Practically sliding.

"If he dings it," Jade said, "I'll end up paying the insurance excess."

"That's it," Cadence said. She reached to the dash and tapped a button.

The sirens burst out. Loud. Piercing.

Jade saw glints on the car's hood from the red and blue rooftop flashers. The engine rumbled. She could feel the urgency vibrating through the seat.

"Hello?" Milton said in her ear.

"Found my truck," Jade said.

"I hear sirens."

Ahead, the truck swung and clipped a parked car. The car tipped. Jogged back onto the curb.

The truck fishtailed.

"There goes that insurance," Cadence said.

"Yeah. I see that."

"What's going on?" Milton said in her ear. "Are you all right?"

"Yes. What did Ealing Cooper say?"

"He knows where the body is."

"The body? As in Rich Cooper?"

"That's right. I think that Ealing thinks he's making a plea bargain."

"Let him. If we find the body, maybe we can tie it back to Ivan Mortowitz do you think?"

Cadence sped on through a narrowing road. Hurricane wire fences around empty properties. A few steel-walled sheds.

Soon even the curbs vanished. The edges of the blacktop crumbled to gravel.

There were still cars parked along the shoulder. The truck hit another one.

"It's like he's aiming for them," Cadence said.

"He is."

The tarmac came to an end. The road turned into gravel. The truck sped on. Ahead, tall trees loomed. The truck bumped and bounced.

"How are you doing?" Milton said.

"It's not getting any better," Jade said.

Just before they hit the gravel, a blue car pulled out from the right. Right in front of Cadence's car.

The blue car braked. Stopped.

Cadence slammed on her brakes. The tires squealed. Jade felt the chug of the antilock.

Cadence steered around. But it was too late.

The cruiser's front fender clipped the blue car. Both cars spun.

Jade's head banged the window. She saw the world whirling.

The cop car slid onto the gravel. Slid faster. Rattled across the shoulder. Came to rest in a ditch.

CHAPTER FIFTY

The world kept spinning. Jade knew the car had stopped, but everything seemed to keep whirling around her. Her head throbbed where she'd hit the window.

She could smell gas.

The car lay at an angle. Her feet fell damp.

"You okay?" she said. Her vision still blurred.

Her feet weren't just damp. They were resting in water.

She looked out the window. There was water there. Brown and weedy. The surface glistened with swirling oil.

Ahead, through the cracked windshield, she could see a pipe. Where the water headed, vanishing under the paved roadways.

She was facing back the way they'd come. In the wreck, they'd crossed to the other side and spun right around.

"Cadence?" Jade said. "You okay?"

"Mm-hm."

Jade looked up at her. Cadence had a cut on her forehead. A black eye. She clasped her left arm across her chest, pressing her hand into her right shoulder.

"You're hurt." Jade unfastened for her seatbelt. The water at her feet rose. It shouldn't be a problem, but they still had to get out. That gas smell was getting worse.

Twisting around, Jade looked at Cadence's injury. Bleeding freely, but clean. It might have almost been cut to the bone.

"There's a..." Cadence trailed off with a grimace. "First aid kit. Glove compartment."

"We need to get out of here." No sense in taping a wound closed if the car caught fire.

No way to open the passenger door. It was down in the ditch. Squeezing up, Jade pulled on Cadence's door handle. It gave, with a quiet click. Jade pushed on the door.

Heavy. Immobile.

The car lay at probably a thirty or forty degree angle. Enough that all the weight of the door, normally borne by the hinges, rested on her hands. And kneeling in an awkward position made it hard.

Cadence coughed. "Let me get my seatbelt off. We can do it together." She grabbed at the release. The belt strained. It held her in place.

The air was becoming stifling. Jade was starting to feel light-headed.

"Okay," she said. "Give me your nightstick."

"Nightstick?" Cadence frowned, making a fresh drop of blood fall from the wound. But she reached down to the side and brought out the foot-long piece of heavy carbonite plastic. "If you catch him, save some for me."

"Sure. Cover your eyes."

Jade stepped back to the passenger door. The water came up around her ankles. She didn't think they would sink, but it was still unnerving. The brackish smell mixed with the gasoline irritated her nose.

Using the nightstick like a battering ram, she jabbed at the crack in the windshield.

The pair made a solid thunk sound, but the crack didn't widen. Jade felt an uncomfortable jarring up her arms.

"Good idea," Cadence said. She continued trying to undo her seatbelt.

Jade drove the nightstick again. Another thunk.

Still no damage.

Again.

Nothing.

The windshield stayed right where it was.

CHAPTER FIFTY ONE

Jade shifted her grip on the nightstick. Her foot slipped against the door. Splashed in the water.

"Keep going," Cadence said. She gotten her belt undone. Now she sat braced between the wheel and the central console. She tried pushing on the door.

"I'm not getting anywhere," Jade said.

She gave another swing. The nightstick thunked.

The smell of gas kept getting worse.

"You'll get there," Cadence said. "We're not getting this door open from in here. She tried pushing again.

"All right." Jade swung again.

Thunk.

Nothing.

Again. Thunk. This time maybe the crack spread some. Around her feet she could see the water bubbling through. She was more worried about the gas leaking. She could see swirls of petrol on the water's surface.

She drove again at the windshield. This time a cracking sound joined the thunk. The crack in the glass spread. Like a map of a river network.

"Almost," she said.

She made another swing. The nightstick thunked into the glass.

The glass shattered. Tiny pieces fell, but most of it stayed together. Bound by some windshield laminate. Designed to bond it together. So that a shattering windshield didn't pepper a car's occupants with shards.

But it was all she needed. The deformation was enough.

Turning in the cramped space, she kicked at the glass. It shuddered. More shards fell. Some of the pummeled sheet pulled away from the rubber molding frame. Another kick and a whole lot more came away.

A hole big enough to get through.

Jade crouched. Pushed her way out.

Standing with one foot on the roof pillar where the windshield's side had been, she grabbed hold of the roof-mounted lights. Scrambling and pulling, she got up across the roof. Onto the driver's door.

A car pulled up. Someone shouted something.

Jade called back for them to come help. She slipped down the door and got her feet onto the bank of the ditch.

Bracing on the back door, she yanked at the driver's door. The guy who'd shouted joined her.

Together they hauled the door up. Pushed it hard.

The hinges creaked. Gave way. The door fell back against the front fender with a clang.

Cadence rose up in the gap. Standing on the console and the wheel. "I had this, you know," she said.

"You really didn't," Jade said.

Together they helped her off and up the bank to the road. They made their way across to the far side of the road.

The sound of sirens again. Coming from the direction of town.

"You know," Cadence said, holding her hand on her injured forehead. "If this was the movies, my car would blow up about now."

"What?" said the Samaritan, suddenly worried.

Jade looked at him now.

Medium height. Medium build.

She'd seen him before.

It took her a moment.

The cook. At the house last night, with the woman. Mortowitz's competition.

The guy met Jade's eyes.

"Thanks," she said. "You make a good chili, I'm guessing."

"What?" Cadence said.

The sound of the sirens continued to increase. Jade saw the vehicles speeding toward them. An ambulance. A fire truck. Light flashing.

"You called the emergency services?" Jade said to the guy.

A shake of his head. "I have a…" he trailed off

with a sigh.

Uncomfortable. "What's up?"

"Ms Howarphe asked me to give you a message."

"Ms Howarphe?" Jade said. Like a little snippet of information. Doled out carefully.

"You met her."

Jade gave him a nod. "I guess the message involves something I should stop doing?"

"No. Something specific to do."

"Mm-hm."

The guy clutched his hands. The ambulance eased by and pulled up just beyond the wreck. The fire truck slowed and stopped just beyond the end of the tarmac.

"What's she supposed to do?" Cadence said.

The paramedics climbed out. They walked toward them. The fire fighters headed on foot toward the wreck.

"Ms Howarphe says," the guy said, "that you should leave town now."

CHAPTER FIFTY TWO

The fire fighters used some kind of foam to hose down the wreck of Cadence's car. Their machinery hissed and hummed. The foam smelled sweet, blocking out the awful gasoline scent in the air.

The paramedics set to work on Cadence's head wound and on her arm. They made her lie down on a stretcher, over her protests.

Milton and Captain Bainer arrived in another police cruiser. A small crowd gathered back from the fire truck.

Jade pulled the guy with the message away quickly. Took him along by the ambulance. "Why didn't she tell me that last night?"

"Things changed. Someone's talking. Things might get bad."

Jade shook her head. "That's not it. She could have left a message with my contact."

"Your contact?"

"I don't need to explain that. You're the messenger. Whatever she chooses to do is her business. Did one of your people steal the truck?"

The guy looked away along the road where the truck had vanished. Bouncing and bumping along the rough gravel. Into the trees there. Eucalypts. Jade saw some smoke rising in the distance, over the high, leafy tops.

"Jade," Milton called across. He headed in her direction.

"Hey!" Jade waved.

"Are you okay? We lost the call."

Jade realized she'd dropped Cadence's phone. It probably lay in twelve inches of water in the car's submerged passenger footwell.

"I'm okay," she said. "Cadence drove just fine."

Milton looked over at the car lying in the ditch. "The captain might take a different view of that."

Another fire truck arrived. It eased its way around the other vehicles and continued on along the narrow gravel road. The new fire truck picked up speed quickly. Dust roiled in its wake.

Jade saw that the smoke beyond the trees was thickening.

"Another fire?" she said. She could hear the crackling of radio chatter from the official vehicles.

"Must be," Milton said.

Out of the corner of her eye, Jade saw a vehicle move. The guy with the message. Backing away. For a moment he seemed to be just getting his car out of the way, but he swept around and sped off. Back toward the highway.

"Did someone get a statement from him?" Jade said.

Milton watched the car departing. "I don't think so. Witness?"

"Yes. He helped us out." Jade explained the guy's message.

"I've got the plate," Milton said. "So we can call it in. But let's get after him." He started toward the parked police car.

The captain hurried over. He asked if Jade was all right, then said, "Someone on a boat on the inlet called it in. Vehicle on fire."

"Vehicle fire," Milton said. He looked back toward the trees and smoke. Considering.

"My truck," Jade said.

"Why?" Captain Bainer said.

"Distraction," Jade said. "Disruption."

"Come on. Let's get down there," Milton said heading for the other cop car. "Let's put a call out on the witness. We'll track them down."

"I know where he works," Jade said, walking with him. "Does the name Howarphe mean anything to you?"

"No."

"She's tied up in all this. Somehow."

Milton and Bainer got into the car. Jade got in back. Milton accelerated away before she even got her door closed.

The car rumbled on the gravel. Milton kept his foot down. Jade could just the back end of the fire truck ahead. Soon they were gaining on it.

"Another fire," Bainer said. He glanced back at Jade through the grate that separated the front from the back seats. "This is turning into quite the week."

He seemed angry. Frustrated.

Jade didn't blame him.

"I hadn't expected this," she said. "Not at all. I thought I was just coming down to help Sebastien with tracking down his uncle."

"No one's blaming you."

"I know."

The car rumbled on. Only a hundred or so yards behind the fire truck now.

The trees loomed. Taller than they'd seemed from back at the wreck. There weren't many. Maybe fifty or sixty. Beyond, more scrub and grasses. Through the trees, in the distance, she could see some kind of white wooden tower. Out on the island. Tollis Island. Where it cut back around Glass Bay.

And something flickering. Closer.

On the near side of the bay.

Fire. Her rental truck.

CHAPTER FIFTY THREE

The fire truck pulled in close to the blaze. Milton swung the police car in behind.

Jade's rental truck stood in a wide patch of open gravel. Flames licked around the tires. The windows were still intact. Jade could see flames inside. The paint on the fender blistering.

"Good grief," Bainer said. "Like I need this." He glanced back again. "Guess you don't need this either?"

"Not so much."

Milton brought the car to a stop. Jade got out. Heat rolled from the fire.

No sign of the driver.

The gravel area led to a rough boat ramp. Jade saw a couple of boats out in the glassy water. She could tell how Glass Bay got its name. The island beyond stood out stark and clear. The sun blazed from the south.

Already the firefighters had hoses laid out.

The connections clanked as they worked with a solid efficiency. Jade figured they were getting plenty of practice.

She saw a flick of light from one of the boats.

She barely had time to think about it when one of the firefighters collapsed.

"Down," she said instinctively. As she ducked she heard the crack of the gunshot.

"What the–" Bainer jerked back. Fell in a heap.

The second gunshot rang out. A second after the bullet.

Another shot. And another.

"Down!" Jade yelled. "Everyone get down. Forget the fire." She moved forward.

Another two shots.

The firefighters were already crowding back behind the fire truck.

One of them stayed with the one who'd been shot. Pressed right down. Lying on the ground.

Another shot.

Firing wild? Hoping to hit something.

Jade kept going. Put the burning truck between herself and the shooter.

Assuming there was just one shooter. Out on the boat.

Jade knelt on the ground. The gravel dug into her knees.

Milton and Bainer took up positions against the cop car. Bainer against the front bumper. Milton back by the door.

"What do you see?" Bainer said.

"From the boat," Milton said.

"Got that."

Milton moved back. He opened the car door. He reached inside. Started speaking.

Radioing it in.

Another shot. Another.

The car's windshield exploded.

Bainer stumbled back. He yelped. Stood.

Exposed.

"Down!" Jade shouted.

Another shot. Wild.

Another.

"Down!"

As Bainer turned back to the car, he jerked. A gout of blood burst from his back.

He collapsed.

CHAPTER FIFTY FOUR

The gravel area seemed suddenly quiet. The fire truck's bright headlights glared. The boat still sat out in the water.

Almost like some idyllic picture postcard. Innocent.

Bainer fell the same way Sebastien had. Lifeless. Bag of bones.

The gravel crunched as Bainer's body hit. Little swirls of dust rose around him.

Milton cursed.

He jumped back around the door. Reached and grabbed Bainer. Hauled him in behind the car.

"The wheel," Jade shouted. Heat from the fire made her skin prickle.

Two more shots.

"What?" Milton shouted.

"The boat's low down. They can fire under the car. Put the tires between you and the boat."

"Got it." He moved Bainer. Straightened him. Checked for his vitals.

Milton leaned back. He stared at Jade.

"We need to return fire," Jade said. "Get them out of here."

"I can't return fire," Milton called.

Another shot.

"Throw me the gun," Jade said.

"What?"

"The shotgun. From inside the car."

"You said stay behind the wheel."

"Yeah. Stay there. I'll come get it." Jade figured she could run.

The boat had to be at least five hundred yards away. A tough shot for most shooters. Moving target.

From a boat too. Even with the water so calm, there would still be some movement. Yaw and pitch.

That's why they were shooting so much. Make up for the shots that went wild.

Jade shuddered. That was how innocent people got hurt. Killed.

"Don't know what you're going to do with this," Milton called. He ejected a shell from the shotgun and tossed it across.

Jade stretched and caught it. Hefty in her hand.

"Ammo," Milton called.

Jade set the gun on the gravel. One at a time Milton hurled across two cardboard boxes of ammunition. Jade caught them both. She pulled the first one open. Loaded three shells into the magazine.

Pulled on the forend. Pumping the first shell back. She listened to the gun's sounds.

She pushed the forend forward. The shell slipped into the chamber.

Jade stood and looked carefully. Through the flames.

The blaze was dying down now. But the flames rose high enough to shield her.

Through the flickering she could see the boat.

Two boats.

One a sailboat, one a powerboat. The powerboat closer. The sailboat with its spinnaker up. Making a run downwind. Beating a retreat.

The powerboat lay at anchor.

"Know what you're shooting at?" Milton called.

"No." She didn't want to fire on some family out for a trip. What if the shots had come from the sailboat? A higher-powered rifle. Better scope.

She couldn't tell what kind of weapon had been firing from the sound. Impossible.

Then, through a gap in the flames, she saw someone on the powerboat's transom. Lying across the boat's passenger couch. A long rod pointing out. Aimed at the shore.

Two thin legs sticking out from the rod.

A rifle. With supports.

That was her shooter.

CHAPTER FIFTY FIVE

The rental truck continued to burn. The fire crackled. There would be nothing left. Even some of the metal parts would melt.

Far off, beyond the grasses to the right, the tip of the sailboat's mast was just visible. Fleeing.

Jade lifted the shotgun. She fired.

Pumped.

Fired again.

Nothing but distraction, she knew. The boat had to be over four hundred yards offshore.

Too far with a blunt instrument like a shotgun. Good if she wanted to bring down some geese or ducks. Or encourage a bank robber to give themselves up.

Effective range maybe fifty, sixty yards.

Not so much for hitting a small, distant target. The shot would scatter across the water. If it even reached that far.

"Never going to hit him," Milton called.

"Nope. But they'll hear the shot. Maybe even see the muzzle flash." Probably not. Not through the flames.

She could hear sirens again. Far too far off.

Milton had gone back inside the cop car. On the radio. Calling the incident in.

Active shooter.

Bainer lay prone on the gravel.

Jade took a couple of steps across. Keeping the burning truck between herself and the water.

One of the burning tires burst. Jade jumped at the sound. Louder than a gunshot. The truck tipped. The paint had almost all blistered off now. Probably not a lot left to burn now. Down to mostly steel.

She sighted on the boat again. Through the diminishing flames.

No one on the transom. The gun had gone.

As she watched, the boat shifted. Started forward. She could just hear its engine.

The bow lifted. The water astern churned. White froth.

The boat quickly rose onto the water's plane. Sped off across the bay.

Jade stepped around from the truck. The boat slipped from view. Just around a slight rise in the ground.

Gone.

She watched the water for a moment longer. Gathering herself. The ripples from the boat's wake faded. Leaving the surface flat and glassy again.

Threat over.

Jade turned quickly. She went to Bainer.

Checked him.

Not breathing. She blew into his mouth. Started giving him chest compressions. Her hand felt immediately sticky from blood.

She remembered seeing the blood burst from his back. A through and through.

Probably not a survivable wound.

She kept pumping. You never knew.

Hard work. She concentrated. Fingers interlocked. Ball of her lower hand against Bainer's sternum. Push. Push. Push.

Training coming back to her. What was the rate again? The beat of some song. Bee Gees. *Stayin' Alive*.

Ironic.

She kept pumping.

"Jade," Milton said.

"Boat's gone," she said. "Shooter's gone."

"Jade."

She was supposed to give breaths too. How many?

Maybe twenty compressions, then two breaths? Thirty compressions?

"Jade."

She was upset. She'd liked Bainer. The picture of his kids. Grady in Nashville with his band. Athena taking pre-med.

"Come on," Jade whispered.

"Jade," Milton said.

"We need a defib," she said, glancing around. "They'll have one on the fire truck."

"Jade. He's gone. The shot went right through him. Through his heart."

"You don't know that."

She sighed and leaned back. She looked up at Milton. "They were waiting. This was an assassination."

"Pretty scattershot," Milton said. He looked weary. Eyes dark. Shoulders slumped. He leaned back against the car. "The guy was firing wild."

"Me," she said. "They wanted me."

"You?"

"Because they think I know what Sebastien knows." Jade looked down at Bainer. His face seemed peaceful.

She stood and headed for the fire fighters. They were clustered around their team member who'd been shot too.

They had some of the victim's clothes stripped off. Jacket and shirt pulled up from her midriff. Blood all over her coffee-colored skin. Bandages going on.

"How's she doing?" Jade said. The woman looked like she was in her late thirties. The beginnings of crows feet at the corners of her eyes. The wound was in her abdomen. Jade saw stretch marks there too. A mother.

Alive, at least. Unconscious.

In expert hands.

Jade walked away. Across the gravel. Toward the boat ramp.

The truck continued to burn. The fire seemed to have found a second wind.

Jade kept walking. Right to the water.

Despite the bay's glassiness, there were tiny waves. Half-inch high. They lapped onto the strips of old concrete someone had laid to make the boat ramp.

The sailboat had vanished too.

Tollis Island lay about a mile away. Two parts of it coming around left and right to form Glass Bay. The southern part, thicker and higher, had trees and grassy swamp. To the north, the thinner, lower part was just visible as a few sandy dunes.

And Jade between the two parts, could just see the far side of the bay. A few buildings there, looking white against a darkening sky. *Bernie's Rest* was among them. Facing out across the Atlantic.

Where had Rich Cooper gone? And why were so many people so interested in keeping it a secret?

"How are you doing?" Milton said, coming up beside her.

"Sad," she said. "How about you?"

Milton didn't say anything for a moment. He reached out and took her hand.

Jade squeezed, appreciating the human connection. It felt oddly appropriate. Not a come on. Just that moment of two people feeling helpless in the world.

"Not like we're dating," Milton said, squeezing back. "Just, well, you seem all alone out here."

"I usually am all alone. Anywhere."

Milton didn't reply.

"The boat went thataaway." Jade lifted her free hand and pointed north. Where the inland waterway lay between the sandy spit that formed the northern margin of Glass Bay.

"We'll never find it," Milton said. "Do you know how many boats there are around here?"

"I'm guessing it would number in the thousands. Even tens of thousands."

"Exactly."

"A process of elimination might give you... what?"

"Well. It was white. But that's ninety percent of boats anyway."

"All right. And it was a power boat. Open transom. Low roof over the wheelhouse. Not really a cabin cruiser, but it would have had a small cabin."

"So now we're down to forty of fifty percent."

Jade sighed.

Milton let go of her hand. He crouched to the water and used it to wash his hands.

Jade looked at her palms. Blood. From Bainer.

She looked back toward the fire truck and the cop car and the still burning rental truck.

"What now?" she said.

Milton stood. "Exactly."

Jade looked into his eyes. "This has to stop," she said.

Milton nodded.

"So, we need to get to work. If you're game."

"What have you got in mind?"

Jade gave him a grim smile. "We'll need some weapons."

CHAPTER FIFTY SIX

An ambulance came. The remaining fire fighters doused the burning truck. The remnants crackled and pinged.

A big yacht tracked across the bay, wake marring the perfect surface.

A coroner and some crime scene investigators arrived. They cordoned and photographed.

Jade gave her version of the story. Milton gave his. The fire fighters gave theirs.

A CSI found a mushroomed bullet inside the police car. The bullet that had shattered the windshield. They found another bullet embedded in the side of the fire truck.

A helicopter with pounding blades flew circuits over the bay and tidal channels. Looking for the boat.

The paramedics checked Jade and Milton's scratches and bruises. A state police officer gave them a ride back to the police department.

Inside, Milton stood at the door to Bainer's office.

"Are you next in line?" Jade asked him. "Acting captain?"

"No. We're a small department, but I'm not in line."

Around the office space, state troopers, plain clothes officers and uniformed officers milled. Mostly engaged in quiet conversations. The smell of bad coffee was almost overwhelming.

"Let's get a car," Milton said. "They're done with us."

"Police, car?"

A shake of his head. "Looks like we're getting short on those."

"Well, no one's renting me any vehicle anytime soon."

"Mine," Milton said. "We just need to get to my place."

"You mean that ancient European thing in your driveway.

"Standard series 3. Nice enough. Does the job. We just need to figure out how to get over there."

"And get it out of the crime scene? I don't think anyone's going to be too worried about your place right now. Not with everything else going on."

Milton gave a shake of his head. "Other way around. More so now. All this is related. Linked together. Bad idea. I could still rent something."

"Good. Okay. I can pay, but I'd better not come into the rental office. Which is good." Jade looked around the busy police office. "I could use a phone."

"My office," Milton said.

"I'll transfer money to your account."

"It's all right, really. I'm not wealthy, you know, cop and all. But I'm not short for getting a rental for a couple of days."

"Sure." Jade smiled at him. She would send him the money anyway. Later. No sense in him being short of cash because of her.

"Go ahead and use my office." Milton pointed.

"I know where it is."

"The rental place is only a couple of blocks off," Milton said. "I'll get someone to drop me and be back inside of a half an hour."

"Okay." Jade grabbed his hand again. His skin felt rough. "Thanks for all this. And sorry."

"Don't you apologize. All of this would have come out sometime." Milton met her eyes. He blinked and looked away.

"I'm sorry about Captain Bainer," Jade said.

A nod. "Thanks." Milton turned and headed for the door without another word.

Jade watched him for a second before heading to his office. She called Angus Webber.

"Another fire?" Webber said.

"I don't know who started it."

"Feels like it's all falling apart down there."

"It really does. In a handbasket."

"Nice turn of phrase. What's your plan?"

"Four leads still. Three here. One who's going to talk. One for you to check on again."

"I might just have something for you there."

Jade waited.

"Madeleine Howarphe," Webber said.

"That's her name. I met a guy. He told me that

she said I should leave town."

"That's the message she gave to me."

"Oh. So she did get in touch with you."

"Yes she did. You could just leave it, you know that? Forget it. It's not like there's any money in it now."

"You know that's not why I do this."

A sigh. Webber said, "Yes. I know that."

Cadence pushed open Milton's office door. A bandage covered the wound on her forehead. Her left arm hung in a sling. She stared at Jade and beckoned to her with the right hand.

"Just a moment, Angus," Jade said. She put her hand over the phone's mouthpiece. "Cadence. Shouldn't you be at home?"

"Can't spare the personnel," Cadence said. The bruises at her eyes looked worse. "Ealing Cooper?"

That's right. "I was going to speak with him."

"I went down there. Tried to get him to talk. Wouldn't say a thing."

"Me?"

"Exactly. He wants to talk with you."

"Milton's going to take me down once he gets a car. Want to come?"

"You bet." Cadence glanced along the row offices. "If I can get out of here."

"Looks like it's all feds now anyway."

"Yeah." Cadence blinked. "I'll let you get back to your call."

"Thanks. Come get me when Milton's back."

"Right." Cadence slipped away, pulling the door to.

"Things okay?" Webber said in Jade's ear.

She took her hand away from the mouthpiece. "Progress of sorts, I suppose."

"Do you have a cell phone yet?"

"No." She had had Cadence's phone for a moment. Lost now, in the creeping ditch water inside the car wreck.

"I might need to call you," Webber said. "Details on these people."

"I'll find one. Milton's probably. I'll call you on it so you'll–"

"Already see him here. Derek Milton. I've a cell number for him."

"All right."

"I don't think there's going to be anything good about them. Howarphe and Mortowitz."

Jade looked up at a knock on the door. Cadence again.

"Someone to see you," Cadence said.

Beyond her stood a trim middle-aged woman. Short-cropped dark hair. White blouse and jeans.

"Angus?" Jade said. "Are we done for now?"

"Yes. I'll talk to you soon. Stick with Milton."

"That's my plan."

Jade hung up and stepped out of Milton's office into the hubbub of the open plan area.

"Emily Jade," Cadence said. "This is Maisie Souther."

CHAPTER FIFTY SEVEN

Officials bustled around the police office. Someone had brought in a big box of donuts and it lay open on shelf behind the reception desk. The donuts glistened and shone and Jade figured they had about as much nutrition as sand, but she still wanted one.

Sugar hit.

Maisie Souther stood in front of her. Probably forty, but still toned. She had a brightness in her eyes that was almost disconcerting.

There was a story about how Maisie ran Gary Petronas's investigations agency with a calm and precise efficiency, while he ran around chasing leads and joining together disparate facts. The perfect operating pair.

Jade held out her hand. Maisie took it and shook. She had a firm grip.

"I heard you were looking for me," Maisie said.

"That's right."

Maisie looked around the office. "We just need a computer. Everything's on here." Maisie held up a tiny memory stick. "Carry it with me everywhere."

"Everything?" Jade said.

The briefest frown crossed Maisie's face. "You want to know about Rich Cooper? About Gary's investigations?"

Jade nodded. "How did you know?"

Maisie sighed. She looked at Cadence. "Is there a computer we can use to access the files?" Maisie turned to Jade and handed her another memory stick. "You can copy the files you need onto this."

"Thanks." Jade took the memory stick.

"Milton's office," Cadence said, pointing back. "I can log the computer to a general user so you can get online and so on, but not at our files. I think."

"Just need to look at these," Maisie said. "And copy over whatever she needs."

Jade liked Maisie brisk efficiency. Not especially warm, but right now warm wasn't what they needed. Information was.

And once Cadence gave them the general access to the computer, Jade saw plenty of information.

Photos she recognized from Sebastien's wall. Documents. Details about *Bernie's Rest*. Police reports which probably should not have been on Maisie's memory stick, let alone in Petronas's agency's possession.

"I've seen a lot of this," Jade said.

"At Sebastien's place?" Maisie said. "Gary said that it got to be a bit like a conspiracy theory museum there."

"Maybe Sebastien had it right."

"Sure. That's not my thing, making those kinds of links. But there certainly is a lot of information. I suppose your questions are about where the gaps lie." Maisie tapped at the computer's keyboard and shifted the mouse. "Let me copy all this over for you."

"Thanks."

The computer screen flashed up with a progress bar as it counted off the files copied from one memory stick to the others.

"Why are you giving me this?"

"Gary. He's taken off. Vanished. After all the shooting, I guess. Doesn't want to get himself shot again. Kind of superstitious that maybe his luck is running out."

"Again?"

"Long story. And nothing to do with Rich Cooper."

"Do you think–"

Another knock at the door. Milton came in. "Hey," he said. "We've got a car. We can go talk to Ealing."

"Good," Jade said. She looked at Maisie. "Want to tag along?"

Maisie gave a firm shake of her head. She pointed at the screen. "This is what I do. Organize the information. I do not go chasing after the guys carrying guns."

CHAPTER FIFTY EIGHT

Ealing Cooper sat in a ragged old armchair in a windowless office in the county hospital.

The only other furniture was a narrow, Formica-topped desk, and an old steel-framed chair that had probably come from a closed schoolroom.

The office looked like it had originally been a storage cupboard. Jade could see holes in the tired gray walls where shelving had once been bolted. From the corridor came the sounds of people moving equipment, having quiet conversations. The squeak of the wheel on a cleaning trolley.

"I'm only talking to the cops," Cooper said. He wiped the base of his nose with the back of his hand.

"I'm a cop," Cadence said.

"Likewise," Milton said.

"I remember you, yeah," Cooper said. "You

were at the fire."

"Which one?"

"The shack," Jade said. She stood in the doorway, behind Cadence and Milton.

"I know," Milton said.

"Her," Cooper said. "I trust her. Not either of you. And you're not even in uniform."

"Still a cop," Milton said.

"Let me talk to her."

"I shot you," Jade said.

"Exactly. That's why I trust you."

Jade saw Milton and Cadence exchange an incredulous look. Jade stepped back so they could exit the tiny office.

"Be right outside," Milton said.

"I'll holler." Jade gave him a nod. She moved closer to Cooper. "You might need to explain that. Trust thing, I mean."

He gave the slightest of shrugs. Some dust rose from the sides of the armchair, motes in the light.

"You have integrity, I suppose. Could have killed me. Could have killed us all. And one of us had shot Sebastien already."

Jade didn't speak. Waited. She could smell the lingering scent of disinfectant. As if left over from when the office had been a cupboard.

"We had some good deals coming along," Cooper said. "Rich said he was going to visit Aunt Nadine. His mom, I mean. No one liked that. We had stuff right there and ready."

Cooper watched her. Still Jade didn't say anything.

"Don't you want to ask me a question?" he

said.

"Why are you telling me now?"

Cooper's eyes flicked to the narrow gap in the doorway. "Rich was blood. Distant, but still family. I see the way the Maeberry family get when one of theirs is in trouble. I'm on the outer there. When they shot Sebastien I felt sick to my stomach."

"But you waited until now?"

"We were all in the same room. What was I supposed to do? Tell you everything then? I'd end up like Sebastien."

"So you're safer in here, but I can't offer. You're not even giving an official statement."

"Already gave one of those. But there's one detail that no one asked. No one even thought I might know."

"So you're telling me?"

Cooper squinted at her. He seemed very young. Out of his depth for sure.

"I don't think you'll rat me out. But I think it's important. Things gotta go better for me. Or they'll go worse."

Jade waited.

"I'm not asking you to help me." Cooper took a deep breath. "I figure I owe it to Sebastien. And Rich."

"Owe what?"

Another breath. "I can tell you where Rich Cooper's buried."

CHAPTER FIFTY NINE

Traffic on Tollis Island was heavy. Surprising. A lot of people making their way to the beach, perhaps.

Oblivious to the dramas unfolding around the area.

Milton drove. The rental car was a little white Malibu. Comfortable seats and sharp acceleration. New car smell.

On the road ahead, two black SUVs sped along. Milton muttered something about external agencies.

"We can't go digging up a body by ourselves," Cadence said from the back seat.

"I know that."

"And remember all the shooting?" Jade said. "We need all the back-up we can get."

"Also," Cadence said, "our chain of command is a mess. And you're technically off on leave. I'm on medical leave already. If we dug anything up, none of it would be admissible."

Milton didn't say anything. He kept focused on the road.

Right after Ealing Cooper, sitting in the hospital's cupboard-office, had given the details on the location of Rich Cooper's grave, Jade, Milton and Cadence had returned to the police building.

The moment they gave Ealing Cooper's details, the feds loaded up in their SUVs and took off.

Jade, Milton and Cadence followed.

They drove beyond *Bernie's Rest*. On past the concrete platforms and holding buildings of the island's small ferry terminal. Gutter Island lay four miles north, across a tidal channel. Some vehicles sat parked and waiting.

Milton followed the SUVs to the end of the tarmac and beyond the last few houses. One last vehicle parked at the road's end. Where the road turned into an accessway out through scrubby pines. A dirt road in worse shape than the one that led to Sebastien's shack.

Soon they came to one of Glass Bay's small beaches. A lot of the bay's shoreline had mangroves. Some of which had been cut back so residents could build jetties to access the water.

A few paddleboards lay on the sand. The three vehicles parked above the high tide line. Plastic shards and twigs and shells lay in a jumbled strip.

Jade walked out across the sand. She could see right away where Ealing Cooper had meant the grave lay. An old picnic table at the edge of the trees, with a run-down slide and swing set.

Beyond those, a path led into the trees.

She pointed.

The group headed off along the path.

Soon they came to an open area. Grassy. The remains of a flying fox set across the far side. The poles weathered and tired, the cable lying curled and rusted across the ground.

"Where is it?" Milton said.

"This way." Jade led them around the side of the open area. Some posts mounted in the sandy soil. Different heights.

"What's all this stuff?" One of the feds said.

"Old confidence course," Jade said.

"I remember it," Cadence said. "I had a cousin who told me about coming out here when she was a kid. There was a summer camp nearby. Wrecked in a storm about twenty years back."

"This is probably all that's left," Jade said.

Beyond the posts lay some horizontal logs. Mostly buried in sand and covered by the ragged grass.

And after the posts, an area devoid of grass.

Sand. With mounds. Low. No more than six or eight inches high. Footprints all around.

"Oh," Jade said.

At least six mounds. Some worn and degraded, with grass growing on them. Some fresher.

One looked only a day or two old. The sand still wet. Clear marks on it from the spade.

Graves.

Not obvious really. Not unless you knew you were looking for someone buried.

"Stop," one of the feds said. "Move back."

"We're entitled," Milton said. "It's still our jurisdiction. Even if we're now assisting you."

"No." The fed took a step back. And another. "There's someone in the trees. We need to–"

The gunshot blew his head in half.

CHAPTER SIXTY

Lying on the old slab of rough wood, Ivan Mortowitz adjusted the big rifle. The cool sea breeze was refreshing. Keeping him alert.

The stunted pines rustled.

People in the clearing shouted. Ran.

Mortowitz smiled.

Take that, Madeleine Howarphe.

If only it had been her. If only.

He fired again. Another one went down.

But now Mortowitz couldn't see any of them.

He'd fired too soon.

He needed to have taken down that woman. The one who'd been probing too much.

Emily Jade.

Mortowitz had eliminated Gary Petronas easily enough

Stupid to have tried from the boat. Too great a range. Too much movement.

But at least that set-up had worked. The kid

with the truck had parked it and set it on fire exactly.

This time that other kid, Ealing Cooper, had screwed up.

Only tell the woman. No one else should have known.

She should have come alone.

At worst, with that cop. Derek Milton.

A mistake to trust Ealing Cooper. Stupid to bring them here.

Big deal.

Mop it all up.

Now it was just a hash. A mess.

A *clustermess,* as Sandy would have said.

So much for her too.

And now he couldn't see any of them.

Still, he had one other option.

There was only one road out of here.

Mortowitz grabbed up the rifle. He slid back along the wooden slab.

Slipped away through the pines.

CHAPTER SIXTY ONE

Jade scrambled behind the closest of the mounds. Itching sand forced its way into her clothes. Damp. It smelled earthy.

Another shot rang out.

The remaining feds yelled at each other.

"Milton?" Jade shouted.

No response.

"Cadence?"

"Still alive. Get down."

"I am." Jade pressed into the sand. Someone buried right there.

Probably not Rich Cooper. Too recent. He'd been missing for a year.

Who then?

"Shooter's on the move," one of the feds said.

"Covering you," another called.

There had been four of them. In their black suits. One dead. Maybe another now.

"What're you doing?" Jade called.

Same shooter as on the boat. But closer now. And without that slight disturbance of being on the water's surface.

"Stay put," one of them called. Scuffling noises as they shifted around.

She rolled. Looked.

No sign of them.

Then a thump from the trees. Someone swore. Movement. Someone pushing through the trees. The swish of branches against clothing.

Moving back across the island.

Jade peered up from the mound.

The two feds had gone. She caught a glimpse of them. Back beyond the confidence course. Running toward the vehicles.

What was their plan?

"Jade?" Milton shouted. "Get down."

"Shooter's gone," she said. She ran around the mounds. Ran into the trees.

There. A slab of wood. Like a table top. Something left over from the confidence course. Or overgrown since.

Crushed grass around the slab.

And then footprints leading through the sandy ground.

"Jade!" Milton shouted.

She started running. Through the trees.

Following the shooter.

CHAPTER SIXTY TWO

The sand squeaked underfoot. Pine branches swiped at her. From the distance came the sound of a boat's horn.

The ferry?

She kept running. Easy to follow the trail. Fresh, damp footprints in the sand. Crushed grass. Broken branches on the stunted pines.

From behind, Milton shouted for her again.

A moving target was hard to hit.

A sniper rifle was a long-range weapon. This was going to be close-quarters.

But she didn't have a gun now.

Bare hands.

She could see gaps in the trees ahead.

The shooter could be lining up on her right now. Taking aim. Ready to take her head off too.

On the ground she saw a piece of timber. A standard length of two-by-four. About four feet long. Lying with some rusted brackets and a couple of other pieces of wood.

Jade grabbed the long piece. Unwieldy. But at least it was something.

Running with it wasn't too hard. She held it near the end. About a foot of it ahead of her. The other end dragged on the ground.

It slowed her down. Not by much.

The shooter had to be carrying a rifle. That would slow them down too.

The boat horn sounded again.

Strange to feel so isolated when there were strangers just over there. Less than a mile off.

She needed to find the shooter.

She kept running. The length of timber was heavy. And getting heavier.

From ahead came the sounds of movement. Still running then. She glimpsed a flash of something. Clothing. Maybe a camouflage jacket.

Head low.

Jade sprinted. Beyond there were vehicles. No. One vehicle. The sun glinted from some silvery trim.

The vehicle she'd seen parked along the road. Before they'd turned toward the beach and found the graves.

"Stop." Jade kept running. "I see you. I will shoot."

The figure burst out near the vehicle. Into clear space.

Kept moving.

Jade sprinted. She hoisted the board. Got it onto her shoulder.

The figure reached the car.

Stopped. Turned.

Brought the gun up.

Jade stumbled.

CHAPTER SIXTY THREE

Somehow Jade kept her balance. A pine branch swiped her face. Needles scratching. Near blinding her.

But she pulled on the board.

She used the stumble. Used the momentum. Used it to bring the board over.

Jade got both hands on it. On the short end. She pulled. Down. Hard.

Her shoulder formed the fulcrum.

The board's long end swept high. Fast.

As the board reached its apex, she thought of the old joke. About bringing a knife to a gunfight.

The guy was steadying the gun.

Last time she'd even forgotten the knife.

And this time she had lumber.

Fast-moving lumber though.

It sliced down. Cutting the air.

Jade kept moving. Barely keeping upright.

The board's end fell fast. It smacked into him.

Whacked the gun right out of his hands. Jammed into his chest.

Fast. Hard.

He slapped back against the car's door.

Jade heard the sounds of breaking bones. Ribs.

The guy coughed.

The gun dropped to the ground. The barrel dug a tiny channel in the sand.

Choking and coughing the guy slid down. Sideways. He landed with his head near the back tire. His face dug into the sand too. Blood trickled from his mouth.

Jade crouched to him. "Looks like you're hurt bad."

He coughed again.

"Want some help?" she said. "Tell me who you are. Tell me why you're shooting at me."

All she got in reply was another bloody cough. Maybe that was all he could manage.

"You've been killing people," Jade said. "Why should I help you out? Looks to me like you've got broken ribs there. Maybe a punctured lung. Probably should get someone to take a look at that."

She stood and looked around. "No one here but me."

"Howarphe," he coughed, barely intelligible. "Madeleine Howarphe."

"Well. I know about her."

"Sent me." More coughing. He spasmed.

Jade grabbed his camouflage jacket and pulled him away from the car. "Gotta roll you over I think. All your weight's going on the broken ribs side." Maybe that wasn't the best thing. Maybe all his blood would run into his other lung.

The feds and Milton and Cadence wouldn't be far off anyway.

The guy grunted as she moved him. Less blood came from his mouth once he was on the other side. Her hand came away sticky from blood soaking through his jacket.

"How's that?" she said. He needed help fast.

Another cough.

"You're Ivan Mortowitz, aren't you?"

He gave the slightest of nods.

"Madeleine Howarphe sent you?" Jade said.

"She's got... dirt on me."

"Rich Cooper?"

Cough. "She had him killed. Found details he'd been... keeping to blackmail me."

"Why'd she have him killed then? Seems like that might have been useful."

A sound from the trees. Milton coming through. The same way Jade had come.

"Because," Mortowitz said, "he had dirt on her too."

"This is the shooter?" Milton said as he arrived. He crouched to Mortowitz. "We need an ambulance out here."

"No," Cadence said, arriving right behind Milton. "Throw him in back of one of the feds' SUVs. Quicker."

"He's giving me information," Jade said.

"No use to anyone if he dies."

"I didn't hit him that hard."

Milton glanced at the two-by-four. He pulled open Mortowitz's bloodied jacket. "Pretty hard, I think," Milton said.

"Yeah."

The first of the feds stumbled around the car, breathless. Jade saw a gull arcing overhead. The bird's head looked back and forth as if assessing the bizarre situation.

Jade stepped back. Let the others take over.

She probably knew enough now. Still some pieces to put together, but she was almost there.

Good.

Just a couple more people to talk to. Gary Petronas.

And Madeleine Howarphe.

Almost there.

CHAPTER SIXTY FOUR

The next morning, Jade sat in Milton's warm office. People bustled around. Feds. Volunteers. Fire fighters even.

It would be a long while before things returned to normal around here. A long, long while.

Outside a squirrel scampered up one of the pines. Full grown trees. Not like the stunted versions out on the island. Jade touched her cheek. Still smarting from where she'd struck the branches on her mad dash.

Milton poked his head in the office. "Did you eat breakfast yet?" He was back in uniform. Leave canceled. Promotion probably coming.

Awful circumstances for it.

"No," Jade said. "I came straight in from the motel." After they'd taken care of Mortowitz, and other formalities, Milton had brought her back to the motel. She'd cleaned up and had a quick lie down.

That lie down had turned into more than ten hours. She'd slept through until five AM. Must have needed to catch up on sleep.

"You won't be sticking around, will you?" Milton said, a rueful expression on his face.

"I'm still here. The case isn't solved yet. You don't know where Gary Petronas has gotten to."

They had Madeleine Howarphe in custody. Ivan Mortowitz had given enough of a statement to make that a necessity.

Plea bargain really.

Looked like he was going away for the murder of Captain Bainer, shot from the boat. And for the federal agent out on the island. And for wounding with intent for the gunshot wound to the other fed.

Still, with the plea, it might be life with parole eligibility after twenty years, instead of life with no parole.

The doctors had patched Mortowitz up at the hospital. Broken ribs, collapsed lung, dislocated shoulder.

There was talk of flying him to Charlotte for surgery. The hospital in Fernville City was already overloaded.

"That's what I came to see you about," Milton said. "They've started exhuming. Looks like eight graves, but there may even be some more."

"Lot of cold cases there, I'm guessing."

Milton shook his head. "Come on, I'll buy you breakfast. I'm just getting in the way here."

"You know something. Tell me now. Don't make me wait until breakfast."

Milton sighed. "The first grave was the newest. Gary Petronas."

"Uh-huh. That's not surprising, I suppose. He was playing both sides."

"Looking out for himself until he looked the wrong way."

Jade grimaced. "That's a terrible pun."

Milton shrugged. "Breakfast?"

"Sure I…" Jade trailed off as a phone rang from Milton's waist.

He plucked the phone out. A little white sliver thing. "Derek Milton," he said into it. Listened. Nodded.

He held the phone out to her. "Call for you. You know you can get one of these of your own? Cheap. On installment."

"I'll bear it in mind." Jade took the phone. Cold in her hand. The screen showed some icons, with the word *BLOCKED* across the top.

"Angus," she said into it. Just like Webber to block his number.

"Hello. Two things. I've found a lot of circumstantial evidence on Madeleine Howarphe. Connect the dots. I'll send it through to the police department. Anonymously."

"They'd appreciate that. Thank you."

"Thank you. It looks to me like there's a federal warrant out on her. The name Howarphe is an alias. That's a warrant with a reward for information leading to the capture of."

"Sebastien would be happy," Jade said. "We got to the bottom of it. Kind of."

"Yes. Now. While I'm talking to you. Have you heard of Wide Notch, Wisconsin?"

"Should I have? Is that on your list of tourist wonders of flyover country?"

"Funny. No. I think we've got a job there. Minor crime ring that's intimidating the local police to the point of paralysis."

"Okay. Good to have something lined up."

"Fine. Call me in a day or two. I'll get you tickets and details."

"I appreciate it."

"Always my privilege. Bye for now." Angus hung up.

"And that was?" Milton said.

"A friend. Handler, I suppose. He finds me work. Helps me look for details on my father."

"You mentioned something about that." Milton glanced back at the bustle of the office. "I've got that car. We should get out of here."

Of course he drove to the same diner. Chakana was nowhere to be seen. As well as the usual crowd of truckers, locals and the same elderly couple, drinking bottomless coffee, a big contingent of out of town law enforcement officials filled the place. A wide variety of uniforms and plain clothes.

A waitress bustled from behind the counter, carrying three plates. The delicious smells of sausage and bacon drifted with her.

"Wait just thirty seconds," she said as she passed in front of Jade and Milton. "I'll find you a table."

"Nothing much available," Milton said.

"Got a table coming free any moment," the waitress called back.

Sure enough a group at the far end, by the

window stood, gathering their belongings. The waitress dropped off the three plates and returned. She guided Jade and Milton through to the newly vacant table. She got them seated as she took the tip and clattered up the used plates into a precarious pile on her forearm.

"Be right back for a wipe down and today's specials." She headed away.

Jade looked into Milton's eyes. He looked both tired and alert at once.

"How long have you been looking for these people?" she asked.

He gave a Milton shrug. It kind of said that he didn't know, but also, did it really matter?

"We got them now," he said. "They'll be sparring in court. Whatever happens, they'll have big blots on their records."

"Yes. You know what surprises me?"

"What's that?" Milton leaned forward.

He leaned back right away as the waitress arrived with a wiping cloth.

Not the same waitress. Chakana.

"You are working," Jade said.

"Well look at you two," Chakana said with a grin. "All busy I bet, but you've still got time to have a breakfast date. That's sweet."

"It's not a date," Milton said.

"Sure." Chakana worked efficiently. Moving the coasters, menus, condiments and specials flyer as she wiped. Done, she laid out fresh utensils from her apron. "What can I get you?"

"Big breakfast," Jade said.

"Likewise," Milton said.

"Predictable." Chakana practically rolled her

eyes. "Back soon. Coffees are on their way." She looked them both in the eye. "I'm hearing all kinds of rumors. From the news that sixteen gang members got killed, to an oil tanker run aground. I guess you two are the ones who know the best?"

Jade did her best Milton shrug.

"Figured," Chakana said, and she headed away.

Milton rubbed his mustache. "What was it?" he said.

"What was what?"

"The thing that surprises you."

"The graves," Jade said. "No one had found them. In all those years. But the mounds were just beyond the end of the road. Someone must have seen something."

"Sure. But who would say? So many people have moved off the island. It's easy enough to get around without really anyone noticing."

"Someone always sees something."

"What I'm thinking," Milton said, "is that they brought the bodies over by boat. Beached beyond the carpark. Dragged them in. Real easy to dig in that spot, since the trees had been cleared for the old confidence course. But it was protected from the elements so the bodies weren't going to wash to the top. Which would happen farther out on the spit."

"Have you told this to the feds?"

Chakana came by with their coffees. "Drink up," she said, once she'd filled the cups. "None of this is going to waste."

"Thanks," Jade said. She sipped. Bitter, as

always. Good.

"Sure I told the feds," Milton said. "And the state police. They're still trying to figure out jurisdiction." Milton leaned forward again. "Did Howarphe and Mortowitz cross state lines with their operations? Or maybe just county lines? The feds kind of want it, but the state police are asking for evidence."

"I can imagine." Jade told Milton what Angus Webber had told her about Howarphe. "Webber's sending the information through."

Milton nodded. "So she'll go away too."

"Yes. I suppose she will."

Jade heard a rumble from the highway. She saw a big pickup. Just like her burned-out rental. But pulling a big aluminum boat on a trailer. Heading for the Atlantic.

Chakana brought their breakfasts. Vast plates heaped with hash browns, mushrooms, sausage, bacon, eggs, toast, tomatoes and spinach. "Right back with your biscuits and gravy," Chakana said.

"It's all right," Jade said, but Chakana had gone. Jade looked up at Milton. "I can't even eat a third of this."

He gave an impish smile. "Do what you can, I'll finish off for you."

"Are you serious?"

Another shrug.

Jade shook her head. She cut into one of the bacon rashers and forked it up. Crisp and perfect. "I'm sorry things got so bad," she said. "Lot of people died in the last couple of days."

Milton looked at his meal. He poked at the egg

with his fork. "I'm going to take that time off now," he said. "Can't be around here."

"I understand." Jade set her fork down. "Vacation?"

A shrug. A just-plain-don't-know shrug. Then, "I'd feel guilty. You know. Relaxing."

"Well," Jade said. "I've got this other thing. Have you ever heard of Wide Notch, Wisconsin?"

"Should I have?"

Jade smiled. "No. I suppose not."

"Well," Milton said, picking up a piece of hash brown with his fork. "Whatever it is, count me in."

###

About the Author

Sean Monaghan has had more than one hundred stories published in the U.S., the U.K., Australia, and in New Zealand, where he makes his home. He has been a finalist for the Sir Julius Vogel Award, and the Aurealis Award. Sean is also a winner of the Jim Baen Memorial Writing Contest.

Acknowledgement

I am grateful to Vera Soroka for her helpful comments and insights on a earlier version of this novel. All the mistakes, of course, remain my own.

Also by Sean Monaghan

EMILY JADE SERIES
Big Sur

OTHER THRILLERS
Ice Fracture
The Room
The Courier
Taken by Surprise

CONTEMPORARY NOVELS
This is the Perfect Way to Wake
Steel Wagons

KARNISH RIVER NAVIGATIONS SERIES
Arlchip Burnout
Night Operations
Guest House Izarra
Canal Days
Persephone Quest

SCIENCE FICTION
Asteroid Jumpers
The City Builders
Athena Setting
The Cly
Gretel
Rotations
Habitat

THE HIDDEN DOME TRILOGY
The Tunnel
The Deluge
The Eye

COLLECTIONS
Listen, You!
Back from Vermont
Balance i
Balance ii
Balance iii
UnBalanced

ANTHOLOGIES (Editor)
Dieselpunk
Hospital
A Butterfly in China

Links

www.seanmonaghan.com

www.triplevpublishing.com

Printed in Germany
by Amazon Distribution
GmbH, Leipzig